The author lives on the edge of the Lake District and was formerly a schoolmaster in West Cumbria, though initially from London. He was an undergraduate at Cambridge and has drawn on his experiences to provide the background to this work of fiction. He has had poems and short stories published and pieces on Radio Cumbria, plus two other novels. His interests include amateur dramatics (he has had sketches performed locally) and playing bridge.

Forty Years On

Anthony Parker

First published in 2017

Parker Publishing

Dedication

To Avril with my Love

Author's note. Though the College has characteristics in common with an actual college, it is a figment of my imagination, and all the characters and incidents portrayed in this novel bear no resemblance to any actual persons or events in Cambridge in the 60s, with the sole exception of the occupation of the Old Schools.

Prologue

Forty years on, when afar and asunder

Parted are those who are singing today,

When you look back, and forgetfully wonder

What you were like in your work and your play,

Then, it may be, there will often come o'er you,

Glimpses of notes like the catch of a song –

Visions of boyhood shall float them before you,

Echoes of dreamland shall bear them along,

Bowen & Farmer

Cambridge, 1965

December nights were always icy cold back then. I crossed King's Parade, much quieter and less brash than today. I must have made my way from the railway station, probably by bus, though I don't recall now. It's just a snapshot; there I was, as if dropped by parachute. The mock Gothic buildings along the frontage mocked the genuine medieval masterpiece of the chapel, but the theme park meme that now feels so strong was absent then. As an eighteen-year-old, naive, overwhelmed, the exact details of the surroundings passed me by. They were just part of an alien world, one I wanted to enter, though with no coherent reason why. If a spaceship had landed on the trim lush green lawn alongside the pavement, and an inhabitant had called my name, I would have registered no surprise.

As I approached the little cobbled courtyard in front of the gatehouse, with its Victorian lights and post-box, I saw another obvious supplicant. He was there with similar accoutrements to me: a duffle bag and a school satchel, and an air of worried bemusement. We were attracted to each other in our apprehension like opposite poles of a magnet.

'Well, this must be the College, I suppose. Has to be, doesn't it, the chapel and everything. I suppose you're here for interview as well.'

I can still hear his voice, nervous and chattering, looking for reassurance and comfort. He was shorter than me, with black unruly hair, and small sharp eyes which glinted in the Victorian streetlight. His accent was a little posher than mine, but still unmistakeably from the suburbs of outer London, from whose rows of redbrick semi-detached houses I had emerged nearly two decades before. He was wearing a gabardine raincoat, in contrast to my more informal duffle coat. He seemed strangely old-fashioned even then; retro my pupils would call it, a throw-back to the fifties.

'Yes, I am. I expect we should report to the porters' lodge. I'm Stephen, by the way.'

'Giles. Pleased to meet you. I'm glad there's someone else to go in with. It is so daunting, isn't it?'

We entered through the postern door set in the huge wooden double gate, with its panelled front and enormous keyhole. It was just large enough to allow one at a time, and we rather awkwardly dithered till finally I took the plunge and went first. The door swung open surprisingly easily, with none of the creaking that one felt an entrance of this age warranted. It was almost too easy, as if I were on a film set and this were the magically opening door to a castle. I timidly entered, stepping carefully over the raised sill of the door. Inside a magical world appeared. Passing under the mock vaulting, in front of us a great courtyard spread out, with a lawn stretching out to a stone statue we learnt later was the founder, one of the Plantagenet kings who came to a sticky end. To our left the gothic fantasy stretched, its fussy arched windows made human by the warm yellow light that flooded out. To our right was the mass of the fifteenth century chapel, tall and sober, the huge stained-glass windows black and forbidding. A few dark figures flit speedily along the paths intermittently lit by the ancient streetlights that lined the court. They all seemed so serious and committed, and old. No students of course, they had all gone down by this time, leaving the college free for the aspirants.

The Porters' Lodge was inside the gatehouse, on the left. The duty porter, dressed in his top hat, looked down on us like a Dickensian magistrate. After we had sufficiently apologised for troubling him, he sought out our details and sent us away to our lodgings, mine in the Parade Hostel, Giles' in the Market Hostel. These turned out to be on the opposite side of the Parade, hidden down narrow dark alleys, with just lettering on the door to identify them. Agreeing to meet up for the evening meal we separated. My room was reached up a narrow dark staircase. The room was a single bedsitter, drably furnished; I remember little of it except the penetrating cold. The only heater was a tiny old-fashioned gas fire with cracked china elements. It generated some heat, provided one was no more than six inches away from it. My abiding memory of that first visit is of sitting in the cold alone in an ancient room waiting for the ordeal to begin.

I summonsed up enough energy and courage to brave Hall for our dinner. Again, I remember little, though I must have eaten the meal. I sat next to Giles; isolated amongst the chattering multitude of candidates, we clung together as if we had been friends for years. Now I realise that everyone in such a situation believes they are uniquely nervous and isolated, but then I felt I had by mistake found myself in the wrong gathering, and that everyone knew I shouldn't really be there.

By the end of the meal I had recovered my self-confidence enough to go for a pint in the college bar, a strange room covered in modernistic murals that I found out later were painted by luminaries of the Bloomsbury Set. The next day we rather incongruously took the last part of our entrance exam: a chemistry practical in which my performance was undistinguished. Next to me was a most confident candidate with an accent that reeked of ancient public school. He exuded the confidence of aristocratic breeding and flew through the practical with aplomb, almost disdain, disappearing with half an hour to spare back no doubt to some ancient ancestral pile. It was the last I ever saw of him.

In the afternoon, I recall sitting waiting in the Gothic confection: an anteroom full of plush chairs velvet curtains and gilt-framed portraits, a stark contrast to my freezing garret. I stumbled my way through the interviews with the Senior Tutor and the Director of Studies. There was just time to say goodbye to Giles, whose experiences I felt had been similar. We parted at the gate, bravely asserting we would meet again the next year in the same place, but not believing it at all...

Chapter 1

Cumbria, September 2010

But we did of course. I had in my hand the photograph that proves it. It's in black and white, specially prepared by the photographer Edward Leigh, framed and embossed with the college crest at the top. Now spotted and yellowing, the faint writing, faded in forty years of sunlight can still be read:

The College Matriculation, 1966

We stood or sat in our tableau before the mock Gothic windows of the Great Hall. There just above my thumb Giles' features could still be made out an inch from mine (Royston to Sawbridge). And there were also Piers and Arthur, but not of course Penny or Jocasta. Inevitably I picked out Huw; his distinctive features seemed to dominate the photograph. These little figures in their long hair and ties smile back at me as if from a distant past, like they were cavaliers or Elizabethans. And like paintings of the long dead they are trapped for eternity, always smiling, always hopeful, no idea of what was to come. Nothing would ever change them; they would always be there, always haunting me. I knew I could never escape those tiny fading images.

I hung the photograph back on its hook; from the engraved outline on the wall it had hung uninterrupted for many years. There was something I knew I'd missed, but that was relevant. I looked again. Of course. It was Huw; he was the only person in the picture not smiling. I went back to my desk. The break bell had just sounded, and through the French windows I could see the boys streaming back noisily and untidily into the house. For a second their blazers and ties, their uniform masculinity connected to the photograph; a throwback to a world now past except in odd outposts like St Breda's. Sighing, I left the correspondence that had triggered my reminiscences and went to do my duty of supervising their consumption of milk and biscuits. I didn't have a chance to come back to it until later that afternoon, when the end of lessons bell had sounded. It still sat on my desk, unmoved, as threatening and appealing as before. I reread it for yet another time.

Dear Stephen,

I am sure this letter will come as a great surprise to you after all these years. It must be over forty. I am amazed I am writing it myself, but when unexpectedly I got the letter which I'm sure you received as well, the invitation to a reunion for our year at the college, my thoughts suddenly went back all that time. Just the mention of the college brought it all back, and once again I think of what happened every day. Perhaps as we get older those early memories become more vivid; I don't know. I realised that I had to see you, and the others, again. Perhaps being back in the college again (they even say we can have our old rooms) can exorcise the ghosts, for me at least. I do hope you can make it; I checked with the college and Piers and Arthur are both down to come, but you were not.

13

Best wishes and kindest regards,

Your old (I hope I can still call you this) friend,

Huw

I put down the letter; rereading it could not change the message. I reached across the desk for my fountain pen – Montblanc, an anniversary gift from my wife – and took a sheet of headed notepaper from a cubby hole in the old Victorian writing desk.

> *Westlake House, St Breda's School,*
> *Housemaster: Mr S P Sawbridge M.A. (Cantab)*

Dear Huw,

> *It was certainly a surprise to hear from you after all this time. Like you, the invite brought back memories that I perhaps would have preferred remained hidden. I was undecided about attending, and most likely would in the end not have done. However, you are probably right; we should try to exorcise the ghosts. This could be the last chance; we are none of us getting any younger, if you'll forgive the cliché. So I have decided to attend the reunion for the 'Class of 66' after all.*

I couldn't think of what else to add. I couldn't bring myself to take up the olive branch Huw offered, nor to refer to any old memories. That just seemed too trite or hypocritical. I thought that with sadness; we had been good friends once. As I pondered, my wife opened the door and poked her head into the study.

'Would you like some tea or coffee, Steve? I'm just making some.'

'Yes, coffee please.'

It was always coffee and so the ritualistic question was quite unnecessary, but I was too wrapped up in my thoughts to make my usual sardonic reply. Sensing the mood, she came inside.

'Is there anything the matter? Has it been a bad day?'

'No, nothing like that. Just got a letter from someone at my college that I hadn't heard from for years. About the reunion.'

'I thought you weren't going to go to it.'

'Changed my mind.'

'Oh.'

There was a long pause.

'I hope that is the right decision. I suppose it will be good to see them all again.'

She left, closing the door gently, and I went back to the letter. I couldn't leave it there. I needed to say something more. Finally, my pen scribed a few more words on the page, and I was able to fold it up, slip it into the envelope, and add it to the pile of House correspondence, to the answers to requests for exeats, and the orders for new carousels.

I look forward to meeting you all again.

Regards

Stephen

I sat back and took it all in. Piers, Arthur and Huw. Names that once were an integral part of my life, but now were banished to an outer memory, so that they hardly seemed more real than characters in a book or film, at least they had been until now...

Chapter 2

Cambridge, October 1966

That first week was a confusion of events and experiences that I can't now put into any kind of order. There are one or two events that stick so firmly in my memory that I can replay them in my mind like a piece of video. I remember my father driving me up with my case and boxes to my accommodation for the first year. It was another hostel, but this time it was out of town, across the Backs, by the Fellows' Garden. Tennis Court Hostel, it was called, appropriately, with the garden on one side and tennis courts covering a huge lawn on the other. It was a modern post-war building in warm brick, utilitarian in style, but softened by oeil-de-boeuf windows and brick pilasters. I believe it won some prize or other. In the background, the tall dark brick tower of the University Library loomed, reminding us all, if it were necessary, that this was a university city. I knocked on the locked door, and was eventually greeted by the warden, an ill-natured fellow who grudgingly showed me my room. It was right by the entrance with a clear view of everyone leaving and entering the building, which I imagined might be an asset in the future.

My father helped me carry my trunk into the room. It had a single bed and wash basin at one end, and an electric fire, a desk and bookcases at the other. The third wall had the windows and the fourth the door and a wardrobe. The remaining furniture consisted of a couple of chairs. The furnishings looked like they dated from the fifties and had seen plenty of wear. Apart from the furniture described the room was completely bare. But it was spacious, light and airy, and outside I could see the side of the Fellows' Garden. My father quickly departed once I had moved all my stuff in; he was always a man of few words. Now came a feeling I can still recall, still experience as if it were yesterday. I felt I was, for the first time in my life, truly alone. Though I had of course been on holiday on my own, in fact literally so when backpacking in France and Spain, I knew I always had the safety net of returning to the family home. But this was not a holiday; this was my new life. I sat disconsolately, feeling like a fish out of water, unable to summon up any enthusiasm. The fact that I had worked so long for this moment made it worse.

For some years, that feeling haunted me, but now it just gives a frisson of horror, as if it were an anecdote that I'd heard about someone else. It didn't last long: a sharp pain of severance that must have passed speedily, for my next memory is meeting Arthur. He was a tall angular lad, with pale almost albino skin, freckles and short blond hair. He was in the room next to mine, also looking out towards the fellows' garden. I must have visited him, for we met in there, but why I can't recall. Perhaps melancholy had driven me out to seek other human contact, or maybe I just felt sociable, that visiting my neighbour was the right thing to do. Snatches of our conversation stick in my mind.

'I'm an organ scholar, that's why I've got this room. It's larger than the others. I need a piano.'

I looked around. The room was indeed bigger, though much of it was taken up with the aforementioned instrument that filled half the room. I smiled, and suppressed my desire to ask him whether it was the college's or his own. A picture came to mind of me and my father trying to unload a piano from his estate wagon, but I suppressed such a thought. We chatted for a while about our backgrounds. Not surprisingly he came from a cathedral choir school and from a musical family. We actually had little in common. I was studying Natural Science and Arthur of course Music. I was totally unmusical; an attempt by my parents to get me to play the violin when at primary school had failed miserably and my audition for the choir at grammar school had ended very quickly. All we had in common was our age and proximity in Cambridge, but that was then enough. We immediately got on well in an undemanding way; both more than receptive to any offer of friendship. I had just found friend number two.

Number three came in the next seven days. They call it Freshers' Week now; I'm not sure what we called it then, but there was a frantic panic to get course books, sign up for lectures, equip our rooms with mugs, kettles and other domestic essentials if thoughtful relatives had failed to do so. There was a Societies Fair where one could join a whole raft of exotic societies. I recall joining the Cruising Club though I had never sailed (and never did throughout my time at Cambridge). I joined the Union, or was it later, and the Folk and Bridge Clubs. Then I met Piers in the college JCR; we collided when on converging courses to the bar.

'I'm so sorry; all my fault. I'm Piers, by the way,' he apologised, holding out his hand. Well, you don't forget a name like that; there weren't many Piers at my grammar school. The next night, he was sitting alone in a cubicle, and our brief encounter was enough for me to offer to join him. The JCR had been recently refurbished in true sixties style, replacing the oddly muralled room in Central Court: all mock leather seats and huge green shaded lights, with bare walls, a huge notice-board at one end, and a long bar at the other. Bare brick framed the exit towards the Hall; we all thought it was marvellous. Piers was tall and elegant, long floppy blond hair hung over his forehead, and he exuded a Chatterton-like aura of forlorn romantic poet. His language and accent spoke of a grand background: Eton, or at least Harrow, and the younger son of an earl. Despite an appearance and manner that seemed typical of one's romantic image of Cambridge, he seemed a bit of a loner. But that really only occurred to me much later; at the time I was mesmerised by this character that seemed straight out of Brideshead Revisited, and was so different to anyone I'd known back in North London. After a pint, Piers suggested we explore a little. We left the college and turned left, heading up Trinity Street. We passed on the right the Whim tea shop, an institution then, set on a corner with a strange Victorian Gothic turret. Piers stopped.

'I often breakfast there; so much nicer than the factory canteen that the college has become. Serves the best coffee in Cambridge.'

I readily agreed, intending to try it sometime, but never did. The free service in the 'canteen' in college was a much more realistic proposition on my grant. It's a clothes shop now. We carried on past Trinity with its huge Tudor gate and statue of Henry VIII brandishing a wooden chair-leg for a sceptre – still there to this day – and then past John's with its patterned Jacobean bricks. At the end of the road we turned left and Piers led me in to one of the pubs on the right-hand side, the Pickerel. It was full of Magdalene undergraduates, many in their distinctive navy blue and pink scarves. Their voices were more public school than at ours. I asked Piers why he had come to this pub.

'My uncle went to Magdalene; he used to bring me here for a meal.'

'So why didn't you go to Magdalene.'

'Oh, too many Etonians.'

The maligned 'factory canteen' brought me my fourth friend. He attached himself to me one breakfast time. The meal was eaten in the Great Hall, producing one of those incongruities that so characterised the College, and upset Piers. We took our trays of food, served by bored staff in a functional server that could be anywhere in the country, out into a magnificent Gothic hall that looked as if it should grace a medieval monarch. It was in fact designed by a famous architect in the nineteenth century, but on a scale that would not have disgraced Henry VIII. There was a stone vaulted ceiling on top of stone columns that would have looked at home in a cathedral. Portraits of past Masters looked down from the wooden-panelled walls; stained glass filled the great mullioned windows. At the end was a minstrels' gallery. I still could not sit without looking up to marvel at the sight.

'What a waste this place is. Monstrous empty Gothic horror, filled with a few scruffy students scoffing lunch. So bloody pretentious.'

I looked around to see who had spoken this heresy. The voice came from a figure to my right. He was almost hunched over the table, his breakfast in front of him, which he was consuming as fast as possible whilst still haranguing anyone within range. Short and stocky, he had straw-coloured short hair that had no discernible style. He wore a dark blue sweater over corduroy trousers, neither of which looked as if they'd recently been washed, and he had a round, rather porcine face that he thrust forward to emphasise his argument, assisted by a fork brandished in his hand. He had a marked Welsh accent that resonated through the draughty empty hall. I can hear it now. We were sat on a long oak bench at an equally long oak table. I mumbled some reply, being a little taken aback by the interjection. Huw took my response for agreement.

'It's good to meet someone else not taken in by all the rubbish. All the phoney traditions, the fake medieval architecture. This university's built on science; that's what we should be celebrating.' Huw clearly had decided I was a kindred spirit, and I did little to disabuse him as he continued.

'Look you, take the chapel now. Have you ever seen such a hideous building, boyo? Looks like a warehouse. And all the rubbish going on inside, all this mumbo-jumbo, pretty singing dressed up as some great uplifting experience. Come to a chapel in the valleys. There you'll hear real singing.'

He sounded like a latter-day Fluellin, if not an Owen Glendower. To dismiss one of the glories of English Perpendicular architecture might seem iconoclastic, but at the time there was a distinct ambivalence towards the ancient buildings of the colleges and university, and some of its traditions. In the sixties, there was still a belief in modernism: many of the buildings then being created won prizes and were much admired, like for example the Cripps Building. Our modern horror of the brutal concrete and glass legacy comes from the way in which those buildings have not weathered well, and the way that particularly residential blocks have proved antisocial. To us in the sixties modern rooms with proper facilities seemed a great improvement on the old, cold and draughty 19th century ones with no bathrooms. We hated Victorian Gothic – phoney and fussy – and only truly ancient architecture, like Corpus Old Court, was accepted by dint of its great longevity. On the whole, I agreed with Huw on the Chapel; it did seem a barn of a building, and since it and the reputation of its music so dominated the outside view of the college many inside reacted against it. I rarely stepped inside, and in fact have entered it far more since than I did as an undergraduate. For not merely did we resent its dominance, we felt we were a new brand of undergraduate. A grammar school generation, many of us from working or lower middle-class backgrounds, like Neil Kinnock, first generation university students, we thought we were the forerunners in a new meritocratic world. So I was happy to listen to Huw, and to accept his invitation to join him for a drink that evening in the Eagle. It was the obvious pub for College men to meet in, being just a hundred yards from the main gate, on the corner of Benet Street and King's Parade. Unlike anything I'd seen before, a galleried inn dating back to the 17th century, its gloomy smoky atmosphere added to the romantic other-worldliness of Cambridge which still possessed me. It was a Greene King pub, and we drank its flagship beer, Abbot Ale, still renowned today, though then I recall I preferred at the time the sweeter, blander taste of Double Diamond. The pub even then was famous for its association with Crick and Watson, who had according to legend announced the discovery of the structure of DNA there one evening in 1953. So a good place for budding scientists to drink, a fact that even Huw appreciated.

'That's the kind of history Cambridge should be celebrating, not looking back to the Middle Ages.'

Giles had just joined us when Piers appeared, on his own. I saw him in a doorway and waved. He came across, a little reluctantly I felt, perhaps apprehensive about my companions.'

'Do you all know Piers? Why don't you get a drink and join us?'

As he disappeared I sensed Huw didn't approve.

'You don't like him, do you, Huw.'

'It's not him, personally, boyo, it's his class. They are the ones that have oppressed the workers for centuries. If they had their way we wouldn't be allowed in here at all.'

I was going to say that seemed a bit harsh on Piers when Giles, who'd previously been quiet, interjected.

'But don't you think that's what they've always done? Let a few talented ones join them, keep the gene pool strong. You think you're blazing a trail for the working class but in fact aren't we just strengthening the establishment.'

Huw for once was struck dumb, and as he tried to formulate a reply, Piers joined us. The serendipity of his arrival with Giles' interjection smoothed his integration, and soon even Huw was laughing at some of Piers' stories about life at Eton. Piers had a knack of making the most mundane detail a source of humour, and his self-deprecating style and obvious lack of awe at the arcane ceremonies of the prestigious public school won over even Huw.

'Not a bad guy for an old Etonian, boyo', he confided in me as we returned from the pub at closing time. The next evening, Arthur joined us. Having accepted Piers, Huw could hardly reject the inoffensive musician, even if he was a 'bloody choral scholar' as Huw rather inaccurately and uncharitably described him privately. So gradually our group coalesced. As I have described it we sound a very disparate collection, with little in common but being in the same year in the same college. But that in fact was enough. When cast adrift in an alien environment, survivors tend to cling to each other, survival being more important than anything else. And I can see now that that is what happened to the five of us.

The routine of our new life started to form about us. We had been sent reading lists including essential textbooks, and we scrambled to get bargains from second-years anxious to recoup their expenditure of the year before. Others we needed to get from the bookshops of Cambridge. They provided a cornucopia of delights to someone whose previous idea of a bookshop was W. H. Smiths. A lifetime's delight in browsing amongst the shelves was kindled, perhaps the greatest legacy I took from my time there. The best was Heffers, in Trinity Street, opposite the eponymous college. It spread out like an Aladdin's cave from a narrow shop front, selling tomes like Roberts and Caserio's Organic Chemistry, costing the amazing sum of £8 then. Trinity Street was a joy, commencing outside Great St Mary's, the University church, with a bookshop whose name I don't remember, but is now Cambridge University Press. It then wound its narrow way, hemmed in by Victorian houses, the ground floors of which were shops like were found nowhere else. I recall there was an excellent sports shop and record store, and a shop whose window was always filled with elegant eveningwear, some so extravagant that only Sebastian Flyte would have dared wear them. There was an ancient church and Caius College, and an inn and hotel called the Blue Boar. Next to it was a kind of steakhouse, which I remember served excellent chicken and chips, the ultimate gourmet experience to our untutored palates. At the far end was a strange gothic court attached to Trinity, where a schoolmate of mine resided.

The lecture rooms and labs for most of Natural Sciences started just the other side of King's Parade, in two complexes known as the Cavendish and Downing Sites. The Cavendish had been the place where the atom was first split by Rutherford and the structure of DNA had been deciphered by Crick and Watson, and so had an iconic and almost mystical status in Cambridge, indeed the whole world of science. But in reality it was a higgledy-piggledy mass of early twentieth-century buildings in red brick mixed in with new fifties and sixties concrete and glass, plus the inevitable porta-cabins. Inside the dull academic corridors and functional labs belied its legendary status. Ironically, the Edwardian brick and sandstone of the comparatively lowly Downing Site was more attractive. The Chemistry Department was quite a distance away reached by a narrow road incongruously named Tennis Court Lane. At the changes of lectures a tsunami of bicycles would pour one way or the other down this lane. Considering the incompetence of many of the cyclists, having cycled little before coming up, it is amazing that I only once saw a serious accident.

Socialising provided regular venues of a different kind. The Eagle, one of the few surviving galleried inns in the country, was a regular spot both for good beer and for a salad bar well ahead of its time. The Indian restaurant in Regent Street and the Chinese in Lion Yard, neither of whose names I remember, were also frequent destinations when dinner in

college palled. The Lion Yard was named after the Lion
Hotel, which I had once visited for lunch with my father;
sadly, it was closed, and about to be replaced by a shopping
centre, so even then I was deprived of its seedy but
comfortable shabbiness.

The college provided an entirely different challenge.
Other aspects of my new life could be related to past
experiences: I had seen provincial county towns and riverside
vistas before and the functional lab complexes only seemed
like grown up schools. But the medieval foundations with
their eccentric arrays of architecture were outside my ken.
The College dated from the fifteenth century, founded in the
reign of Henry VI, not perhaps the best of inspirations as he
was both insane and ineffectual. The architecture told the
history of the college over the intervening years to the present
day. The oldest part was the great chapel on the North side of
the front lawn, its magnificent perpendicular windows and
vaults the pride of Cambridge. It was all that was built of a
grand design, the rest abandoned when Edward of York spoilt
the party. Down the South side stretched Benet's Building, its
Victorian Gothic confection fooling many a tourist, and as a
total contrast the modern development of the Crane Building,
all sixties concrete and steel, a brutalist fantasy. Joining the
two was the Georgian block called Grange, a series of
staircases once occupied by fellows, but now mainly offices.
Down at the bottom next to the river was Bradley's, an early
twentieth century accommodation block for third-year
undergraduates of undistinguished appearance (the building
not the students, or not all of them anyway). Beside it
stretched the great back lawn running down to the Cam,
which together with the end of the chapel and the back of

27

Grange makes up the iconic view of the College so familiar in the media. Even today when I see it as a back drop for an interview in some current affairs programme I feel a jolt; whether of pleasure or pain I'm not quite sure. My attitude to it all varied from a cowed feeling of awe to a proprietal pride in being part of it all.

Each evening we ate in Hall, still formal at that time requiring gowns to be worn. Though the days to having to wear gowns in the streets after dark had gone, that had been a recent development, and gowns were still an important part of our everyday lives, being worn to dinner, when meeting tutors, for exams for example. There was a hierarchy of gowns. Scholars wore a distinctive long gown. Exhibitioners, a kind of minor scholar, wore their own type, and commoners, the rest, including myself, wore a short gown. Perhaps because of that, and maybe also because of the sixties' mood of rebellion and challenge to authority, most of us disliked wearing them and tried to avoid them as much as possible. I remember one of my year getting around the Hall rule by draping himself in a black curtain; nobody seemed to notice or care. Fortunately, as scientists we were not expected to wear gowns to lectures and practicals, I can't recall now if arts students still did.

The food in Hall did not sadly stand up to the formality and setting; the three courses seemed always to start with a version of brown Windsor soup. The portions were not large either, and some of us developed a plan to increase the quantity by fifty per cent. The college servants brought the plates of food in threes, and one plate would be hidden under the table to be shared out later. No one ever seemed to catch on, or else they didn't care. Most college servants had been local, but many were Spanish in my time. Now I would imagine they were East European. Hall was the communal occasion of the day, the one time when all undergraduates, having returned from lab or lecture room or library, met together as a body. So of course, did the fellows of the college, parading through the lines of hungry undergraduates to their place at 'High Table' on the raised dais at the end of the hall. In those days most ate in college, and I can still recall images, the former Master Doggart stomping in what sounded like hobnail boots, and the iconic figure of the great novelist, J. M. Taylor, tall, bent and exceedingly old. He lived on A staircase, next to the Hall, in a room off a corridor that seemed the height of a cathedral with a gothic pointed arch for an entrance. It's a graduate common room now. Huw, Giles and I always sat together; Huw had decided he had found in me a bosom pal, probably because I suffered his iconoclastic outbursts more than most others. Giles and I had almost telepathically agreed to face Hall together from the first day, as if our embryo friendship the year before had cemented our relationship for all time. More often than not Piers joined us, until even Huw accepted his presence as part of college life, even if their relationship was still a little frosty, myself being the common factor. Arthur too joined us if not with the other musical scholars.

'Spending all my time with music makes eating with it too much', he confided in us. 'It's all talk of what anthem will be played in chapel, and how a choirboy sang a note too sharp in practice. But I suppose it would be the same if you scientists just talked about catalysts and molecular theory.'

Indeed, it would have, and one of the reasons we jelled as a group was our ability to escape the strait jacket of the subject. I suppose we lacked the true dedication, the singleness of purpose that makes a brilliant academic and was to make some of our contempories Nobel prize-winners and the like. Our conversations ranged over a wide field: home, arts, rock music, but most of all politics. It was of course the time. The Wilson government had been elected with an increased majority, and there was much talk of a new age. Social attitudes and customs were changing in the 'Swinging Sixties' and most of us felt we were entering a new meritocratic age forged in the 'white heat of technology'. But for many Wilson's reforms were too slow; they wanted full-blooded socialism, and believed the time was right. And in the East, the Vietnam War was raging. I had been a Labour Party member before coming up, but soon realised that to some that was almost a betrayal.

'You must realise, Steve, that tinkering will not do. The establishment will not change otherwise. They'll pretend they have, but they'll still be in control.' I can still hear Huw's voice now.

Often we would continue our discussions over coffee in one or other of our rooms. We were all in the same Hostel which made it easy. I try now to think back to what we discussed, but all I can recall is a series of unresolved disputes. In the Middle Ages students would sit on the 'Tripos' and dispute on religious topics. For us politics was the new religion, and we disagreed and disputed long into the night, never coming to a conclusion, and rarely I imagine changing minds. The main protagonists were Piers and Huw, the former saying less but speaking with an authority that even Huw recognised and respected. I liked to have my say, but Arthur and Giles generally preferred to listen, especially

Giles. He hung on Huw's words, until I felt he was becoming almost an acolyte. It worried me sometimes; he seemed to take seriously some of the wilder ideas that we came out with, which now seem quite lunatic, and even then I took with a large pinch of salt.

Chapter 3

After a while other students started to refer to us as the 'Famous Five', after a series of popular children's books of the time. Though probably meant disparagingly, we started to revel in it; it gave us an identity and bound us together. The Famous Five in Enid Blyton's imagination were always going out and engaging in adventures, so it seemed natural that we did the same. We all had bikes; I had brought mine from back home, old but serviceable. Piers had inherited one; it looked like an heirloom passed down through generations of Piers. Grand but battered, it seemed a metaphor for the aristocracy we believed Piers to have originated from. Arthur had purchased a sturdy second-hand one, and Huw had 'liberated' one from its capitalist owner, at least for the day. But Giles' one was the star. It was brand-new, with shiny handlebars and a multiplicity of gears linked to an arrangement of chains whose understanding defeated the most physically minded of us.

'It was a present from my parents for getting into Cambridge. They promised me a new bike as my reward.'

We were split between abhorrence of such a bourgeois gesture and envy of the shining contraption. It was felt after discussion that we would not regard his possession as a class betrayal, but worthy of a decent outing. It was a Saturday morning; we had finished a leisurely breakfast in hall, there were no lectures and we were clearly in need of something to do. Piers first suggested it.

'What about a visit to Ely?'

It was a good suggestion. Ely lay to the north, across the fens, an easy ride but far enough to feel we were escaping

Cambridge, heading out into the unknown. Piers spoke of its famous 'Cathedral of the Fens', and won Huw over with promise of good pubs and talk of Hereward the Wake, the rebel against William the Bastard.

'O.K., boyo, you've talked me into it. Come on, lads, let's get going. The pubs will be closed before we reach Ely.'

We set out from Cambridge, riding in line. Piers, as the unofficial leader, led, his hair streaming behind him, sitting up in the saddle and looking back to shout some unintelligible comment carried away on the wind. Behind him, by grace of his new bike, rode Giles, upright and proper, like a newsreel of training police motorcyclists I once saw, all earnestly weaving in and out of traffic cones. I came next, and then Arthur cautiously gripping his handlebars. Tail-end Charlie was Huw, hunched over the frame, pedalling furiously to keep up with his longer legged companions. Soon we were well clear of Cambridge, through Chesterton and Milton and Waterbeach, and then we were on the Ely Road, the A10. But Piers took us off down country lanes and out into the fens. We were cycling through a weird landscape, the like of which we had not seen before. The land was totally flat, with the strange water channels called drains that gave the area its distinctive nature regularly cutting through the fields. Where they flowed to we did not know; most were dark, muddy and torpid. Ancient sluices with rusty gates operated by keys were everywhere, but we saw not a soul. There was no sound beyond us; just the occasional cry of a bittern. It was late in the year, and the sky was steel grey, with just a few fluffy clouds scudding across the heavens. There was a biting wind from the North-east, straight from the steppes of Siberia, but we battled on. About half way, Piers stopped, and we each drew alongside.

'Look at that.'

We followed his arm. Wherever we had looked before the flat fenlands stretched remorselessly, out to the horizon, but now rising out of the grey back ground like some giant spaceship loomed the tower of Ely Cathedral. As we cycled the church gradually grew nearer as if it were drawing us magnetically; our limited conversation tailed away, and we cycled relentlessly towards it.

We reached Ely just on lunchtime, and found a small pub tucked away in a narrow lane near the cathedral. I tried to find it on subsequent visits, but it seemed to have disappeared like a JK Rowling invention. It comprised a series of narrow rooms, with ancient beams and low roofs. It was crowded and hot, smoky from nicotine fumes which had stained the walls and ceiling a rich brown colour. All the rooms were packed with men who looked like farmers and spoke with a distinctive East Anglian accent which we found difficult to follow, but they seemed to be discussing the price of sheep and the direction of the weather. Eventually we managed in one of the furthermost ones to find a table free. We were tired but warm from our exertions, cheerfully buoyed up by the collective pleasure of our friendship and our achievement in escaping from Cambridge.

'A pint of beer for everyone?' Piers as our unofficial leader offered to buy the first round.

'O.K. boyo, I'll have a pint of Abbot Ale.'

Huw rather truculently selected the strong local ale from Greene King. I opted for a pint of Double Diamond, a sweet keg beer very popular then.

'I'll just have a coke. I'm not much of a drinker.'

Huw snorted at Giles' response, but said nothing. Arthur joined me in a Double Diamond.

'You don't seem to like Piers too much, Huw,' said I, rather provocatively as Piers fought his way to the bar.

'Nah, I don't mind him; it's just the born to rule thing all his class have.'

'Born to rule?'

'Yes, you all accept him as the leader; he steps in to get the first round and we all defer to him.'

'I didn't notice you rushing forward to offer. And you were happy enough to accept.'

Huw snorted at that.

Any further discussion was curtailed by Piers' return with the drinks. Huw busied himself with rolling a cigarette, the tobacco and paper extricated from an old and battered tin that looked as if he had inherited it from his grandfather.

'Why not try one of these, Huw?' Piers was holding out his packet, Dunhills I think, or some such expensive brand. Huw snorted.

'I'm OK with my roll-ups. That's what we smoke where I come from. Care for one?'

Piers dismissed with a smile the offered tin, and proffered his packet to me. As I accepted one I caught Huw's eye. He had a look of triumph. I felt myself blush a little, and tried to redeem myself by offering a light for the three cigarettes. The other two turned down the two offers.

'You know it ruins your health,' piped up Giles, ignoring the black looks from the three smokers.

'I can't smoke; it ruins my singing,' stated Arthur.

'I thought you were a bloody organ scholar.'

'I am, Huw, but we are expected to sing in the choir as well.'

Huw muttered something like 'poncy mumbo-jumbo', but we all ignored him. There was a hiatus now; and each of us drank our drinks, and waited for someone to break the silence.

'So, what do we all think of Cambridge so far?'

It was Giles who spoke first, nervously articulating what we had all been wondering; were our impressions the same as the others. There was another hiatus. I answered him first.

'I didn't know what to expect. It's so different to what I've known up to now. These fantastic buildings and the sense of history; it's overwhelming. You just feel so insignificant and unworthy. All the famous men who've been here. I do wonder sometimes if I belong.'

'Bollocks,' said Huw, draining his pint as we sat spellbound at his blasphemy. 'It's all phony, a pretence. Look you, the fellows push their rules and regulations, just to keep us in our place. Most are less than a hundred years old.'

'Things are changing; we no longer have to wear gowns after dark.'

'Huh, anything like that would be unthinkable at any other university. This place needs a revolution, throwing out all these outdated traditions, and making this place a modern university, dedicated to serving the whole community, not just a few rich tossers.'

'Why did you come here, then?'

'Cos it's the best for science in the country, and despite what the toffs may think, we are all entitled to the best.'

No-one answered him at first; then Arthur piped up.

'I think it would be a pity if all the old traditions went. That's what makes the place different. And then there's the music; it would be tragic if the choral tradition disappeared.'

'Spoken like a true organ scholar,' scoffed Huw. 'So what do you think, Piers? You haven't had your say yet.'

He just smiled.

'I think you need another pint, Huw.' Huw grinned rather grimly and held out his glass.

'I need to go to the bog.'

Piers got up and turned to us, but we, embarrassed, indicated our lack of desire for more refreshment. Piers disappeared again towards the bar. In their absence, Giles turned to me.

'His egalitarian principles don't stop him taking drinks off Piers.'

'No, true. There's quite a bit of hypocrisy there. But he does have a point. This place should be for everyone if they're good enough. But you haven't said what you think either.'

'I don't really know what to think. Like you, I'm overawed by the power and beauty of the place, but it never seems real, does it? Maybe Piers finds it natural; those who've been to famous old public schools, but it just doesn't seem real. Will we get used to it; will we look back in the future and take it for granted? I don't know.'

'What is real? Do you think having been to places with the same old turrets and soaring spires makes us believe that this is normal?' Piers had returned and was looking challengingly at Giles and me. 'Believe me; you will never take this for granted.'

Huw returned and I was pleased to see that even he showed a little embarrassment at accepting Piers' generosity. A barmaid appeared suddenly at our table with a large plate of sandwiches.

'Was it you what ordered these?' She plonked them down on the table and disappeared leaving us speechless.

'I thought we needed a little sustenance for the journey home.'

Piers brushed aside our indignant offers to pay, whilst Huw, of course, immediately tucked in. They were good sandwiches: egg, beef, ham, cheese. I suddenly realised how hungry I was. I ate a couple then jumped up.

'We'll get in a final round, come on, Huw.' I didn't give him much option, but practically dragged him up and to the bar. It was hot and smoky away from our little nook, and the bar itself was lined with local farmers, but we eventually got the attention of the same barmaid and ordered another round. I didn't really expect Huw to contribute, but to my surprise he dug deep in his pocket and contributed a couple of florins to the round.

'You shouldn't just take from Piers, you know. You're exploiting his generosity.'

'Oh, these rich guys have lots of money. What we have to live on is just pocket money to them.'

'How do you know that's true? We get decent grants; we're not short of money.'

And that was true. Not merely was our tuition paid, something we never even thought about, but we received a grant for living expenses. It was means-tested, but if made up by one's parents, as mine was, or if on the maximum, as I suspected Huw was, one could live very well. Huw did not respond to my comment, but just picked up a couple of the drinks and went back to the table. When we'd finished our pints, and eaten the sandwiches that Piers had managed to persuade the landlady to make, we wandered outside, meeting the shock of the cold air after the fug of the bar. It was still quite early; the sun hadn't set though a steely appearance was creeping into the sky. We agreed almost without speaking to make for the Cathedral, our college scarves wrapped tightly round our necks. It was still open, and we slipped inside. There the strange mixture of overpowering silence, the smell of dust and incense, and the variegated light from the setting sun through the stained glass left us temporarily wordless. We slowly permeated inwards, looking up and around us. There was almost no-one else present, except someone who from his garb was clearly a cathedral verger of some kind. His rather pointed and disapproving expression either suggested a disapproval of young casual visitors, or a desire to clear the cathedral and go home; I couldn't decide which. Arthur picked up a guidebook.

'Listen to this. The cathedral was started in the 11th century. It was a monastery until Henry VIII. Of especial interest are the decorated Lady Chapel and octagonal lantern.'

'What's an octagonal lantern?' asked Giles.

Before I could hazard a guess Huw took an interest.

'I'll bet the peasants who built it were starving whilst the rich abbots and bishops spent all their taxes on wining and dining.'

Before I could comment that I thought monasticism was supposed to be about poverty, the verger loomed up, gliding noiselessly in his long black robe like a ghostly monk.

'You do realise that you are supposed to pay for that,' he hissed, pointing at the guide book. Huw snorted and walked away muttering something about Church wealth and exploitation. Shamed, Arthur and I dug out some silver from the depths of our pockets and inserted it into a slit in the wall marked Cathedral Funds. Smiling at the verger, whose air of disapproval did not waver an iota, we beat a quick retreat and set out to find the aforementioned Lady Chapel.

The sun had long set when we finally emerged from the church. Arthur looking back said 'It's grand but not as grand as the Chapel.' We nodded agreement with a proprietorial air. It was starting to darken as we set off back towards Cambridge. Gradually the sky blackened, lightened only by the faint glow of the distant lights of Cambridge. We cycled towards them. Somewhere we took a wrong turning. Gradually we realised we were all alone. There seemed to be no-one else around, no houses with welcoming lights, no cars or other road-users. The ghostly white shape of a barn owl swept suddenly across our path and nearly caused me to fall off. We were cycling harder now, with an intensity almost bred of fear, as if some nameless dread was at our heels, invisible and silent but there all the same and slowly catching us. Even Piers was bent forward, out of the saddle, as we raced along beside an extra wide fen whose water now seemed black as ink. We cycled in line, each intent on his own endeavour. Then it was totally dark, an enveloping black darkness barely penetrated by our weak cycle lights. Gradually we were spread out, the others barely visible to me. I looked back for Huw, still at the back. I realised with alarm that I couldn't see either him or his light. I pulled my bike up and waited and listened. Not a sound. Then I just caught what sounded like a cry. It was so faint and brief that I thought I had imagined it. There was nothing more, and I had just persuaded myself it was a barn owl when I heard it again, a brief sound that disappeared on the wind, but which I knew this time was real and sounded like a cry of 'Help'. I turned back and retraced our steps. It didn't take long to find Huw; he had come off his bike, and was sitting on the ground holding his ankle. Despite his obvious pain, he hadn't lost his acid tongue.

'Trust you to come back for me; you wouldn't get the aristocrats doing it, would you? It's good old working-class solidarity.'

I just smiled at his response, and felt the errant ankle. He flinched, but I couldn't feel any break.

'Must have hit a bump, or something. Lucky not to go in the drain. Think I've broken it?'

'No, I don't think so; I reckon it's just sprained. Can you get to your feet?' I helped Huw get up. He gingerly put some weight on the dodgy ankle whilst I picked up his bike.

'I can't cycle. I'll have to walk back.'

'Rest your weight on my shoulder.'

So we slowly made our way back. The night was impenetrably black now. I was pushing the two bikes, their feeble light just enough to keep us out of the drains. I was beginning to get tired and cold myself, even under my breath cursing Huw and his ankle, when we heard voices in the still night, and saw faint lights erratically winding towards us. It was the other three.

'What's happened to you?'

'Huw fell and twisted his ankle.'

For once Huw was unable to raise a comment, and he didn't demur as Arthur and Piers supported him whilst Giles and I looked after the bikes. It was late when we got back to college, and we'd missed Hall. Piers as always took command of the situation.

'You get Huw back to his room, and I'll arrange some food for us.'

I don't know how he arranged it, but soon we were all eating soup and sandwiches in Huw's room. No-one worried about how they'd happened, not even Huw. After a few minutes of scoffing – none of us realised how hungry we were – Huw suddenly broke the silence.

'You know, I'm really grateful for what you all did for me out there. That was real friendship.'

'Well, we couldn't leave even you out there on the fens,' I said flippantly, but inside Huw's words had warmed me. Looking around, I realised we all had a little glow of satisfaction. The incident had bound us together: a male bonding that superseded our feelings of awe and inadequacy. We were not just isolated individuals; we were a team now, musketeers together. We could face the future with confidence; we were no longer alone.

Chapter 4

The friendship and bonding that had strengthened through
our adventure undoubtedly improved my ability to cope with
the strange society we had found ourselves in. First was the
need to accept that our pattern of life had irretrievably
changed. The lack of the stabilisers that most of us had relied
on up to now - family, school, neighbours and neighbourhood
– disconcerted most of all. I spent many evenings just
wondering or cycling around, trying to get to know
Cambridge, experience the flat countryside with its huge
fields of arable crops, and even come to terms again with the
dreary fens. I put off initially exploring those wet, dingy
lands, but when I did, either in the company of one of the
others or on my own, I started to discover a strange love for
them. The loneliness and solitude seemed to penetrate my
soul in a Wordsworthian sort of way. In time the wildness,
the eerie cry of the curlew, the impenetrable blackness of the
drains and the sturdy wild flowers growing on the dykes
actually made the fens become a thing of beauty. Some
evenings I would cycle out and turn off on to narrow country
tracks running beside channels filled with the black still fetid
water. I would carry on till there was no-one else around, no
stocky grim-faced women in utilitarian coats heading home to
cook their husband's dinner, no fishermen trying to entice
some inhabitants from the vasty deep. Eventually I would be
totally alone, just miles of boggy fen under a slate grey sky. I
stayed till I'd had enough of solitude, enough of being a loner,
and needing company again. Then I'd climb on my bike and
return, feeling perhaps that I was beginning to think of

Cambridge as being home, being a place I belonged, if only in contrast to the deserted wilderness I had just left.

By the middle of term, I was well into the routine. Each morning I'd cycle across to the Cavendish or the Downing Site, depending on my lecture pattern, and when my first had finished, I'd often join the peloton of cyclists hurtling down Tennis Court Lane towards the Chemistry labs in Lensfield Road. Afternoons would often contain practicals at the same sites, separated from the lectures by lunch usually taken in a pub; mostly we didn't return to college. In the evening, we would usually have a tutorial, or supervision as they were called. Outside of the formal part of university life we drank pints in the bar or the Eagle, coffee in each other's rooms, or watched a small black and white TV in the college's one dedicated room. As a treat, we'd go to one of the cinemas in town, the wide screen in full colour such a contrast to the TV mentioned above. The favourite was the Arts Cinema, down a narrow alley from a shopping street off the Market Place. It showed foreign and cult films, and we all thought we were great intellectuals watching such films as 'Belle de Jour' and 'The Seventh Seal'. We did frequent the main town cinema which was opposite Christ's College; I think it's a supermarket now; I remember seeing 'Yellow Submarine' there. But generally, looking back now, those days all meld into one. Actually pulling out one from the mass, like taking a file from a cabinet, is very difficult, but there were days that stood out, and that are ingrained in my memory separate from the common herd. I recall that one evening there was a reception for newcomers to the college hosted by a college officer. He was a bachelor don, one of the few still living in Grange, in the white stone building that blocked the view of the river from the front lawn. We entered his quarters on the ground floor from the dull and somewhat dinghy staircase, passing through an anonymous and unadorned wooden outer door and then a green baize outer to enter a world I could not have imagined. The large living room was the size of a small classroom, and looked out through two full length windows on the front lawn and the gatehouse. The opposite side of the room had two doors into what I imagined were a bedroom and study. I had been in similar rooms in other parts of Grange, which mostly now were offices, but this was unique. The walls had bookcases up to the ceiling and everywhere were rare and beautiful Persian artefacts stunningly displayed: porcelain, sculpture, tapestries, rare books and prints. I can see the picture in my mind now. There were some older members of the college present, all talking with the same accent and engaging in esoteric conversations of the kind I only ever met in Cambridge, never since. Many of us were overwhelmed and retreated nervously to the outer reaches of the gathering, holding our drinks firmly and feeling totally estranged.

'This is weird; are these people real?' said Giles.

Arthur knew some from the college music. 'Most of them are OK when you get them away from this kind of gathering.'

'But it's so unreal. No-one talks like this elsewhere.' But as I said that, I knew I had to accept this as part of my new world. Only Piers was enjoying himself; I saw him deep in conversation with an elderly don known for his liking for young men.

'He's in his element, Piers. I wonder he bothers with us; he's so different.'

I agreed with Giles with a nod, but didn't really believe it. There was something about Piers that was insecure, needy even. He needed us as much as we needed him, his confidence in this setting notwithstanding. As if on cue, Piers came across, the elderly don in tow.

'May I introduce three of my friends: Stephen, Arthur and Giles.'

We all shook hands and mumbled greetings.

'And where are you all from?'

Naively, we related our geographical locations, but it soon became apparent that what the savant was interested in was where we were schooled. The grammar schools that Giles and I professed clearly disappointed him, and only slightly was he mollified by Arthur's middle ranking provincial public school. He changed tack to asking us what we studied. Giles' and my Natural Sciences again disappointed him. After a few desultory sentences he drifted away, glad no doubt to escape our philistine influence. With relief, the three of us took the opportunity and slipped away, out through the green baize, into the staircase that seemed even more bare and dusty now. Giles and I went down into the front court, while Arthur descended to the basement where the only ablutions were, as indeed was true of all the pre-twentieth century buildings. He came out speedily, blushing a crimson shade across his cheeks.

'You'll never guess what someone's just suggested to me down there!'

We both laughed at the thought of the innocent Arthur being propositioned in a college loo, and the three of us proceeded towards the bar. Before we again entered the college I looked back. The bright lights glowed almost red from the room we'd just left, standing out from the dark court barely illuminated by the decorative but ineffectual street lamps that lined the front court. Virtually all the rest of Grange was in darkness; the room we'd just left seemed like an outpost of the old Cambridge in a philistine new world. I knew that this would be an evening I'd remember, that the strange idiosyncrasy that was both the college and the university would stay with me in such memories, and that it was possible to come to terms with it.   We crossed the court into the college bar. With its garish green light shades, its carousels with plastic seats and a long bar lined with the pumps of the popular beers of the day, it could not have provided a starker contrast. We found Huw sitting in one of the carousels. He had not bothered to go to the reception. Gathering pints from the bar we joined him.

'Well, boyos, you didn't stay long. Not your scene?'

His Welsh lilting voice still sticks in my mind. 'Not really, a different world.'

'It makes you feel you don't belong,' piped up Giles, who had been very quiet all evening.

'Nonsense, man, they just want you to think that. They want to keep this place to themselves.'

'They?'

'The establishment, the privileged, the rich. They don't want grammar school boys like us intruding. But we are the future, lads. Times they are a changing. Stand up to them: don't play their game.'

I wasn't totally convinced by Huw, though I could see what he meant. I felt it was more an inertia, a world changing too rapidly for some, and I was sure many of those talking eruditely about obscure Persian poetry and regaling each other

47

with anecdotes about hilariously nicknamed dons would have been horrified if they realised how excluded some felt. But I knew we had to accept that Cambridge would always be very different to the redbrick municipal universities we had rejected. Always Brideshead rather than Lucky Jim. I tried to convey that feeling to Huw. He wasn't having any of it.

'But there are young fellows who are quite different. No 'them and us', no perpetuating the old hidebound ways. Really radical. As committed to the cause as we are. Come to the Socialist Society, I'll introduce you to them.'

Much later we left the bar merry and in much higher spirits. Before we went back to our rooms, Huw pulled me aside.

'It won't change on its own, you know. We've got to make it change, both here and nationally. Run it for the benefit of the proletariat, not the bourgeoisie and the rich. Come with me to the Socialist Society; you'll meet others who think the same way and want to do something about it.'

I wasn't so sure. I had met some of the more prominent left-wingers, of which there were quite a few in the college, which had a reputation for being more radical than most. They were responsible for the giant red hammer and sickle displayed at one end of the bar. I was far from sure about such gestures. A visit that summer before going up to Yugoslavia and Rumania had left me very sceptical about communist regimes. Also despite Huw's comments I noticed that many of the most enthusiastic socialists were from some very prominent public schools and what seemed to be privileged backgrounds. Plus ça change. But I didn't want to disappoint Huw, so I said I would accompany him to the next meeting.

After the night of the reception life went back to normal. It was remarkable how quickly we had all adjusted to new routines, the lectures at nine, practicals at two, tutorials at seven. But then in many ways it was like school, albeit with no parents to chase us out of the house, or teachers to ensure we did our work. And for natural scientists there was plenty, with four subjects (for me physics, chemistry, maths and cell biology), practicals in three of them and supervisions in all. Those of us who were scientists and engineers begrudged the humanists their more leisured life; I recall one even managing to miss an evening tutorial because he was still in bed. But the more intense routine that we had did have its compensations; the camaraderie of the laboratory led quickly to friendships. And so another brick in the wall was added.

Chapter 5

I'd noticed the two girls before; they'd been in the Chemistry lecture the previous day. It wasn't that surprising I'd noticed them; there weren't many girls doing Natural Science in those days. The few that did tended to stick together and sit at the front. But now these two were on the bench next to me. We were working in pairs, and I was working with Giles. The task was preparing some organic compound. I don't recall exactly what, but it involved lots of interconnected glass that looked like something out of Frankenstein's lab, all bubbling and hissing away, until at the end some oily, aromatic liquid emerging. Or at least that was the idea.

'You're not having a lot of success, are you?'

One of the girls was speaking to me. She was a tall, rather willowy girl, with a complexion like a china doll and long blond hair tied in a pigtail hanging half way down her back. A real English rose. Under her white lab coat she had on a white blouse that was almost translucent, showing her bra beneath which enclosed a pair of small breasts. She was wearing blue jeans nicely pressed: a girl who believed in dressing well I thought. Her accent was Surrey stockbroker belt, and she had that special confidence that only pretty, well-bred young women exude. I was delighted that she spoke to me: strange when you think about it, since the same comment from a man would have been an insult. But I took it on the chin; even being spoken to by such a vision was a compliment. Being such a beauty amongst so many men meant eyes followed her wherever she went; every man on the course must have dreamt of dating her.

'No, practicals are not my strongest point.'

This was absolutely true. I always was amazed when I managed to produce something that looked at all like the expected result. I had nearly ruined my chances during the entrance exams when in the Chemistry practical the crystals I was supposed to be making turned out to be a dirty green powder. Perhaps that's why I changed to IT after leaving Cambridge.

'Why not have some of ours? We've got loads.'

I looked across. She and her partner had indeed produced a large quantity of the aforementioned oily liquid. It seemed rather a cheat, but we did need to do tests on our product. I looked back at our bench. Giles was desperately heating a flask, still clearly hoping that something would manifest itself by magic from the white bubbling liquid.

'OK. I'll take you up on that. That's kind of you. I'm Stephen, by the way?'

'I'm Jo, short for Jocasta, dreadful name isn't it, and this is Penny. Good to meet you.'

The reply came not from the vision but from her partner, who was busy collecting the precious product. She was almost the exact opposite of Penny. A few inches shorter and quite a few pounds heavier, she was curved where her friend was straight. The contrast extended to her colouring, which was dark to Penny's light. Long, curly black hair which fell in ringlets over her shoulders, deep brown eyes, a face not pretty, but with a welcoming smile. There was a guileless openness about her, and an air of energy and enthusiasm; I guessed she had done most of the work on their bench. I took the hand she proffered, which was warm and

surprisingly strong in the handshake, and then shook hands
with Penny, a languid hand, cool, almost ethereal.

After the handshake there was a nervous hiatus, which
I broke.

'Well, we'd better get back to work.'

'Here's your diethylate,' said Jo, offering the oily
liquid in a flask. I took it back to the bench. Giles was not
impressed.

'It's the technique that is important, not getting the
result from someone else.'

But when the graduate demonstrator came round to
see how we were getting on, Giles said nothing as I proudly
proffered our results.

'Well done, Sawbridge. Last time I came round you
seemed in some trouble.'

I caught Jo grinning out of the corner of my eye, and
smiled back.

At the end of the practical, I invited the girls to a
drink at the Spread Eagle, a hundred yards from the labs down
Lensfield road. It was lunchtime and I often popped in for a
quick sandwich rather than going back to the College. It was
a strange little pub, a narrow low building sandwiched
between two larger ones, a kind of conservatory jutting out
into the street, with a huge black eagle on top. It's still there,
though now it has some silly name, like the 'Slug and
Lettuce'. Giles had disappeared back to college to write up
the practical, leaving me to entertain the girls. They sat each
nursing a half of bitter whilst I consumed a pint. I ordered
some sandwiches, hoping that my investment might prove
worthwhile.

As we sat I couldn't take my eyes off Penny. She had that blonde beauty that was so in vogue in the sixties: all those pictures of slim boyish figured girls in miniskirts that so typify the age. She was definitely in that mould, and played to the image: the epitome of cool. She sat, totally fresh and fragrant in that smoky, hot pub atmosphere, like a rare orchid. I can not only see her now, but smell her, almost taste and feel her; the memory is as clear as it was forty years ago. Rather tongue-tied, I resorted to talking about the work we had just been doing. Looking back, I realise she must have been bored, sitting there with a pleasant but disengaged smile on her face. But just to have her attention was sufficient.

'So how are you enjoying Cambridge? Have you done much?'

Jo showed no reluctance to talk. Indeed, she must have generated most of the conversation that day. Unlike Penny, her bright dark eyes engaged mine as she leant forward to ask her question. She had an engaging smile which I now realised showed interest in me that was quite lacking in Penny. A strange but not unusual triangulation: my interest in Penny, Jo's interest in me, and Penny's interest in... Penny?

'Yes, I think so. It's strange: so different from what I'm used to or expected. I've made a few friends. We cycled over to Ely together last weekend.'

'Oh, that was nice. Did you have a good time?'

'Yes, mostly. But one of us fell off his bike and twisted his ankle.'

'Oh, that was a pity. I hope he's OK now. We've made lots of friends too, haven't we, Pen?'

Penny gave a regal smile of approval, and Jo, encouraged by the endorsement went on.

'We didn't know each other till we got to New Hall. We're sharing a room; I was really worried when I heard that was what happened, but then when I met Pen I was so delighted. We are so lucky; we get on so well, don't we?'

Penny nodded amiably, but not quite so enthusiastically, I felt. After finishing our drinks, we walked back into the laboratory courtyard, and retrieved our bikes from the frames. Jo's was new but cheap:

'Daddy bought it for me when I got my place at New Hall. I couldn't do without it.'

Penny's in contrast was somewhat ancient but good quality. I guessed, accurately as I subsequently discovered, that it had belonged to an older sibling, her brother. But she didn't volunteer the information, and so we mounted our cycles, and headed back into Trumpington Street towards the centre of Cambridge. I left them at The College dismounting to walk through the college. They shouted something indecipherable as they cycled on, and I watched them go, Penny upright, effortless, almost regal, whilst Jo pedalled away furiously to keep up.

I realised I was smitten, and spent the rest of the day thinking about Penny. Her cool looks crept into every unguarded moment, and I found myself dreaming about taking her out, sitting by the Cam, cycling together through the countryside. Strangely, these were very innocent day-dreams; no sex was involved. It was almost as if Penny was too pure for that, like a Pre-Raphaelite beauty. There was something almost medieval about her. I couldn't imagine sleeping with her; it would have been sacrilege. It is an easy cliché to talk of worshipping someone, but in Penny's case it was almost literally true. I had led a pretty sheltered life until then, in terms of women. Despite the image of the 'Swinging Sixties', the reality was that most of us were still virgins, regardless of what we might brag to others. I had been educated at an all-boys grammar school, which was excellent academically, but which discouraged contact with girls. So by the time I reached Cambridge my experience of women was almost none existent. Penny and Jo were the first girls I had met outside my family other than in forced social situations: church hall dances and the like. Therefore, though I longed to ask Penny out, I was far too timid, and far too frightened of rejection. To actually ask the goddess and be rebuffed would be too much of a humiliation; it was preferable to worship from afar, as if in some magical way we might suddenly fall in love, like Snow White and Prince Charming.

I saw her of course at lectures and practicals, and sat near her sometimes, and discussed lectures and assignments, and joked about our efforts in the labs. I felt I was getting to know her better, but our friendship was only developing platonically; I was far too inhibited to do anything but hide my feelings. But I knew I was not alone. There was plenty of opposition from other Natural Science males. Jo and Penny were, as I've stated above, part of a tiny minority of women in the department, and they always had men hanging around them, like young stags at a rut. If they ever needed any help with an experiment, at least half a dozen men were ready to step in and assist. I used then to think how lucky they were, but now I can see the disadvantages to being subject to such attention. With my mind on the girls and coping with everyday life, I had little time for Huw and his revolutionary tendencies. I put off going with him to the Socialist Society, and we seemed to drift a bit apart. I spent more time with Piers. He had sought me out the evening after the reception as I was having a drink before going into dinner.

'You didn't stay too long at the Dean's last night. Not really your kind of show?' His comments mirrored those of Huw, though coming from the opposite direction.

'No, they all seemed in their own world. I felt rather out of it, as did Giles.'

'Ah, don't let them fool you. They are no more superior intellects than they are Martians. Anyone can speak on an obscure topic, and seem wise beyond the dreams of Solomon, but the trick is to have your own topic. If someone is talking about the Odes of Horace, I counter they cannot match the poetry of Omar Khayyam, or vice-versa. Just have some obscure subject to hand that you know more about than anyone around you, and you'll always be in command.'

'But it's not just their intellectual knowledge; it's all the people they know, and can quote.'

'Don't be fooled by that either. Many are notorious name droppers. They often have come no closer to them than standing beside in the urinal. Don't worry, after a year or so you'll be name-dropping as keenly as anyone.'

Almost without realising it I found myself being drawn into Pier's social circle. It was wide and amorphous. He seemed to know a great number of people; if we were walking down the street he would regularly be calling out to someone on the other side of the street, and they would reply, both speaking in the same accent. He noticed my look and smiled.

'It's being at Eton, it marks you for life. You can always recognise a fellow old Etonian.'

But it soon became clear that despite this pool of acquaintances he had few real friends. His greetings were often superficial, and I came to realise that we four were probably as close to him as anyone. I asked him one day why he didn't have any close school friends up at Cambridge when there were so many old Etonians here.

'I did have a close school friend, but he died.'

I didn't raise the topic again. The term flowed by; we were into the last couple of weeks. I still had not really developed a pattern for my life at the College. Penny seemed as far away as ever. The friendship with Piers had reached a plateau of intimacy; there was a wall I couldn't climb over. I of course went to the lectures, practicals and tutorials set, but I was just following the path set out for me, like a railway engine tied to its track, only able to go one way. But before I could determine a path for myself, an incident sent me in a new direction.

Chapter 6

One evening after Hall, when I had settled down to tackle some supervision questions, Huw came around to my room.

'I must talk with you.'

I invited him in, and brewed up some coffee in the gyp room. But before I could serve it he was at my shoulder, excited to tell his news.

'Have you heard what they've done?'

'What who've done?'

'The Plantagenet Society.'

'Oh.' I could guess what he had to say. I'd heard about the Plantagenets soon after I came up. They were an exclusive dining society with a reputation for rowdy behaviour. Their members were generally wealthy and well-connected, with the Boat Club well-represented, rather out of line with the College at the time, egalitarian and unsporty. Their name referred to the founder of the college, Henry Plantagenet. Generally, they did not affect other members of the college, except in terms of noise and rowdiness late at night. Depositing items on the head of the Founder's Statue on the front lawn, upsetting a few chairs, throwing up in the courts, that sort of thing but rarely much beyond that, and most college members regarded them as a mildly irritating anachronism at worst.

'It's outrageous; they think they are living in the nineteenth century. That this is still the preserve of the rich. They go as if nothing's changed.'

'So what have they actually done?'

'Not merely have they trashed the JCR, but they've wrecked Pete's room. Scattered all his notes and records, apple-pied his bed.'

I could see now why Huw was so upset. The trashing of the JCR was par for the course for the Plantagenet, like their antics with the Founder's statue. But going into another student's room was another matter. There was always a delicate stand-off between the 'hearties' of the Plantagenet, generally right wing, and the left-wingers, who in those days were far to the left of New Labour. Indeed, they were to the left of Old Labour too, many being Marxists and Trotskyites. Whilst on the left myself, I had little sympathy with the most extreme of them, regarding them as egoists and fantasists. Peter Benson was one of their leaders, and a constant critic of the Plantagenet. But his opposition had little effect on the Society, and it seemed strange that they should target him. Whatever their motive, they had broken an unspoken rule of the College; that one did not victimise another College man. I knew some action would have to be taken.

'Yes, that's going too far.'

'We have to take some action. There's a JCR meeting called for tomorrow evening, after Hall. I trust you will be there.'

The meeting was held in the Curwen Room, adjacent to the court of that name, a strange Victorian Gothic concoction of pointed windows and turrets, which seemed to typify the Plantagenets. They seemed then, I recall, out of kilter with the spirit of the age, when modernity was king and the 'white heat of technology' was going to lead to Utopia. The room was packed, with most standing, and I could see that both sides of the College were represented. The Left were out in force, forming a solid, disciplined phalanx on one side of the room, their casual attire – jeans and sloganned tee-shirts with Che Guevara well represented - marking them out from the Plantagenet and their supporters, many in Boat Club blazers and bow ties. I saw that Piers and Arthur were on the periphery of that group, whilst Huw was prominently next to the phalanx. I felt a pang of anxiety that the 'Famous Five' was already fragmenting, and resolved to stand somewhere near the centre. I saw Giles there, and went across to join him. In the chair for the meeting was the President of the JCR, a third-year who belonged to neither faction. He struggled to bring the meeting to order.

'We are here today to hear complaints from some of our number regarding the recent behaviour following a Plantagenet Society meeting. I call on Peter Benson to speak first.'

Peter then spoke, outlining, with a remarkable lack of rancour, what had befallen him. His speech was greeted with great cheering by his supporters, and some applause from the uncommitted. It was followed by the president of the Plantagenet, who again was conciliatory, expressing his regret at the incident, and saying it was an individual act. I could feel the tension dropping, casual conversation was breaking out and some were drifting away. The meeting was almost done when Torquil rose to speak. Torquil Baron-Smythe was one of the grandest undergraduates, an Old Etonian from a titled family, rather a throwback to an earlier College. When asked why he had chosen the College rather than the more aristocratic Trinity or Magdalene, he always replied that his forebears had been undergraduates at the College since the eighteenth century and he was not going to break the tradition.

More relevantly, one of them had been the founder of the Society. He was a tall gaunt character, dressed in a colours blazer and a purple and white bow-tie. Even then, he looked a throwback to the past.

'I fail to see why so much fuss is being made about a harmless prank. Those in the corner should develop a sense of humour. In fact, the humourless attitudes of some in the college are in total contradiction of its traditions. But maybe that's to be expected, now that admission to the college seems to be open to anyone. No wonder standards have fallen.'

Mayhem broke out in the room. Everyone was shouting at once; the phalanx advanced towards Torquil, who retreated rapidly amongst the Plantagenets. Fortunately there were enough people to interpose themselves between the two, who shouted insults and offered challenges from a safe distance. Then the phalanx started a chant:

'The workers united will never be defeated.'

It seemed rather strange to me on reflection, as most had probably not done a day's work in earnest in their lives. But at the time I was as incensed as anyone; all of us from grammar schools felt a little like interlopers in this strange world that the grander undergraduates inhabited so well, and the last thing we wanted to hear was someone making that public. So I was angrily shaking my fists at the bowties and shouting abuse with the rest of them. At the height of the uproar, I saw Huw jump on the chairman's table.

'Comrades, we have heard enough. The Plantagenets must be banned, here and now.'

A great roar of approval was matched by cries of outrage from the Plantagenets. I heard shouts of 'Commies', 'dictatorship'. Then I saw Piers up on the table. He raised his arms almost in a Christ-like gesture, and amazingly the hubbub subsided.

'Fellow College men, I speak to you as someone new to the college, and not aligned to any faction. We have two important principles to remember here. The right to freedom of speech and association, and the right to privacy and peace. Both are likely to be broken in this week. The behaviour of the Plantagenets towards Peter must be remedied; I suggest a case of good champagne. You can afford it.'

As the laughter died down he went on. 'But the Plantagenets should be allowed to continue, but only if they become more democratic. Let those who want to join, let us all know what you are doing, join the rest of the college, stop thinking you are a special elite. I come from as privileged a background as anyone here, and I regard no-one my inferior; in fact, I could wish I could match the talents of many here.'

It all sounds corny in retrospect, but it carried the meeting. Most were ready for a compromise, and Piers' speech was greeting with cheering. Initially the phalanx tried to continue the resistance, but seeing the meeting was against them, they retreated from the room in good order. The Plantagenets looked relieved, like French aristocrats told they were facing a strict talking-to instead of the guillotine. As everyone filed out, I caught Piers' arm.

'That was a great speech. You changed the meeting.'

'It was nothing; someone would have said it sooner or later.'

'I'm not so sure about that. So, will you join the Plantagenets under the new regime?'

Piers smiled and pulled me towards him. He whispered in my ear: 'I'm already a member.'

'Good lord, were you at that meeting?'

'Yes, but I didn't take part in the trashing of the room. That was Torquil and his mates. I don't think I'll be very popular with them for a while. Even for them a case of champagne costs a good bit.'

Someone else grabbed Piers and pulled him away from me, and I wandered out into the bar. There Huw was holding forth. As he saw me he broke off and came over.

'Well done, boyo. We showed those rich prats, didn't we? Come and join us for a drink.'

I accepted his invitation and wandered over to his group. There was an assortment of members: some other first years, some broken off from the phalanx, some I didn't know. The talk was of triumph and vindication. I sensed that all were, despite their bravado, a little surprised that the Plantagenets had been humbled. It seemed to mark a turning point, and to be honest I was quite pleased. Despite being one for live and let live, the existence of an exclusive club thinking itself beyond the rules of the college rankled. Suddenly I sensed someone at my shoulder, and turned to see Giles. I had forgotten about him in the excitement of the meeting, but he must have followed me out. He seemed a little strange: flushed and tense.

'Hi, Giles, what did you think of that?'

He turned to me with a strange expression.

'We grammar school boys must stick together, you know.'

I looked at him without speaking, and he went on.

'They don't really want us here, you know. Oh, they pretend, all these public-school types, and the fellows with their strange accents and weird ideas, but they really wish we weren't. Oh course, they need some of us to keep up the standards and to pretend that the university really is a meritocracy, but that's not what they really feel. It's like the party in Grange; we all felt it then, didn't we.'

I didn't know quite what to say, and he turned away. 'I must go off to my room; I have a practical to write up,' and he was gone.

The conversation left me troubled. I knew that like most people I wanted to belong to the society I was living in, and I was angry with Giles for raising my own fears. I turned back to Huw and his crowd.

'Do you think we really have established ourselves? Are we really setting the agenda here, or are we fooling ourselves?'

Huw came across and put his arm round my shoulder. 'Of course we are; we are the masters now. We are the majority, and soon public schools and privilege will be things of the past. You see, the world is changing. It's like Bob Dylan says: "The times they are a-changing,", "don't block up the doorway don't stand in the hall". It'll be a new world, and we can do our bit here and now. Look you, things are going to change in this university, you wait and see.'

I was inspired by his words and went away quite uplifted. But once I was back in Garden Hostel, lying in bed and listening to some drunks, with familiar posh accents, carousing outside, I wondered how different things would really be.

Huw had decided, after the Curwen Room meeting, that I was a prime target for recruitment to the Socialist Society. After much prodding, I eventually agreed to go. I can remember nothing about those meetings, except that they were very boring, and what action there was mainly consisted of different factions fighting for control. They must have made some impression on me, because I recall going to a couple of demonstrations and handing out pamphlets. That all sounds very radical now, and maybe somewhere I appear on some ancient file on student activists, gathering dust forever in some government archive. But the reality was that I regarded it as just a social activity, with the beer afterwards the most important part. By the end of my time at Cambridge I had severed all links, but only after the occupation.

It was I who got Giles involved. Now I realise how unwise it was. To survive the Socialist Society you had to take it all with a pinch of salt. There was always a touch of the Citizen Smiths, suburban revolutionaries, about it, and the vehemence of some of the views expressed could carry one along for a while, till you got back to your room and came home to reality. But Giles couldn't do that; everything was real and literal to him. I think now he would be thought of as autistic, but then he was just one of a number of slightly strange personalities in the college; none of us really thought of ourselves as ordinary.

Chapter 7

Cumbria, September 2010

'Are you sure you've got everything, darling?'

'Yes, I think so. Even the college bow-tie.'

'Is this a good idea? Wouldn't it be better to let sleeping dogs lie?'

'Maybe, but I feel I've got to go. I need to know.' I gave her a peck on the cheek. 'You sure you'll be O.K. here?'

'Yes, of course. Mike's coming in to do the house duty, and the boys are all out playing cricket or running and jumping somewhere. We'll put on a film for them tonight. Just go off and enjoy yourself.'

She smiled and I kissed her lips before getting into the old Volvo. I watched her standing in the colonnaded entrance to the house as I pulled off down the drive, the gravel crunching under the wheels. "Just go off and enjoy yourself". It wasn't quite what I was expecting. In fact, I was not really sure why I was going at all, and just as I was coming up to the M23 I nearly turned around and went home. But I couldn't do it. I realised now that I was drawn on, both by a consuming curiosity and a need for expiation. What would they be like, how had it affected them, how had they all turned out? And could they say anything, offer anything that might finally get rid of the guilt?

The M23 fed into the M25, and for a while the ferocious traffic consumed all my attention. But once I was on to the M11, and heading North past the familiar towns of Bishop's Stortford and Saffron Walden, the congestion eased, and I was back with my thoughts again. I felt the strange feeling I had when I first went up, and as I drove through the familiar outskirts of Cambridge, I realised I actually felt nervous and shy. How would they all react to me? Had they kept in touch? Was there a network I was completely unfamiliar with? I came in on the Madingley Road, and turned off down Grange Road. It was as peaceful as it had ever been, with its big Victorian houses set back behind screens of trees, the college playing fields, and the ugly functional building of the Real Tennis Court. Suddenly a half-forgotten memory came back to me...

There was a party in the Tennis Court. It was late in my first term, a strange place to hold one perhaps, but there weren't that many rooms outside colleges that were large enough for a big gathering, and this was a big one. It must have been someone's 21st birthday, I don't recall who. I nearly didn't go; I had a practical to write up, and a supervision to prepare for. But, bored and unable to concentrate, I put my work aside, got my cycle out of the rack, and set out.

It was late when I arrived. The court itself was converted into a dance floor and was in pitch darkness, just illuminated by some flashing lights on the disco. The room was filled with couples mostly closely intertwined. It was obvious that most people had paired off, and, unable to recognise or talk to anyone, I adjourned to the temporary bar, set up in the viewing gallery just off the court. There was the usual student party array of cheap wine and beer bottles; I grabbed a bottle of ale and stood looking out on to the dance floor. Once I got used to the darkness, I could make out some of the figures in the room. A couple I recognised from the College, also a couple of natural scientists; the women I didn't recognise, but imagined they were probably nurses from Addenbrookes: the usual source of women for parties in the female-lite university. Then I saw her, crossing the room and coming straight towards me.

'Hi, Steve. Fancy seeing you here. Pete invited me, but I don't really know anyone, so it's good you're here. Are you enjoying it? I do like the music.'

It was a girl I'd met briefly at the Cambridge Folk Club. Anne, I think was her name. She'd told me she was a nurse at Addenbrookes, on the surgical ward. I'd quite fancied her, but been a bit too timid to take it any further. She was wearing a white dress, high-necked and bare-armed, and very short. The dress was tight and showed off her figure. She came close, and I could smell a mixture of cheap perfume and sweat. In other circumstances, it might have repelled me, but instead I was aroused; there was something primeval about it all.

'Come on, let's dance.'

Without waiting for a reply, she grabbed my arm and pulled me on to the dance floor. We found a small cavity in the array of entwined couples, most of who seemed to be practising mouth-to-mouth resuscitation. We entwined ourselves, and she immediately placed her face next to mine. I held her a little more tightly, and was rewarded for my audacity by her hand around my neck, running her fingers down my back. Almost automatically our mouths met. Though a virgin, I had at least kissed a couple of girls, but her open-mouthed kissing was of a different order. I felt her thrusting her leg between mine, and, as I knew I was aroused,

I felt immediately embarrassed, but it was soon clear that she was not deterred. Gathering courage, I slipped my hand on to her breast. This was a bit daring for me, as a similar manoeuvre at a party back home had led to a face slap, but that night I felt her hand drift down between my legs, its goal very clear. I felt a mixture of excitement and fear; no petting had ever gone so far and I knew she wanted to take it further. She grabbed my hand and pulled me towards the exit. 'Come on, let's go somewhere quiet.'

We slipped out of the court building, and across the road, down towards the pavilion on one of the college playing fields. As we reached the building she slipped round the back, delved behind a rainwater barrel and emerged with a key. She unlocked the front door.

'Should we really be here? Aren't we breaking and entering?'

'Don't be such a goody-goody; no-one will know we're here. And we can hardly be breaking in if we've got in using a key.'

We went into the darkened room, just lit with moonlight. There were photographs of old college teams round the walls, which gave a ghostly feel to the place. It felt like there were hundreds of eyes watching me. But she was not affected by the atmosphere. She leant back against the snooker table in the middle of the room and pulled me onto her. As we kissed more I felt her undoing my belt and zip and slipping her hand inside.

'Come on, let's do it.' She slipped off her pants and leapt up on the table, opening her legs to me. I climbed up on top.

That first time was all over very quickly. I stammered an apology.

'Don't worry, we can't hang around here anyway. Someone else might have the same idea.' She jumped down off the table and pulled her knickers on.

'I got carried away; I shouldn't have taken advantage of you like that.'

She laughed: 'Don't be silly; I made all the running. It's not the first time I've been here.'

I should have realised that. How would she have known about the key otherwise? But the matter-of-fact nature of the encounter didn't bother. For the first time the sexual permissiveness of the Sixties had become manifest in my life. I was elated; I'd broken my duck!

'I'm sorry; I didn't have any er... protection.'

'Don't worry, I'm on the pill, but,' she said, squeezing my arm, 'And don't worry, I won't expect you to make an honest woman of me. I've got a boyfriend back home anyhow.'

'I'll walk you back to the nurses' hostel.'

'You needn't, I've got my bike. I love the way you're such a gentleman.' She squeezed my arm, and we had a moment of intimacy more genuine than what had gone before.

'I'll cycle with you.'

'You don't have to.'

'I want to.'

'That's nice.'

Suddenly we both simultaneously stopped speaking and froze. There was no doubt; someone was outside. It sounded like a couple of men; they obviously had a legitimate right to be on

the premises as they were talking quite loudly. They came up
on to the veranda.

'That's funny, the door is unlocked.'

'There's no one about, no lights on.'

'No-one who should be here, that is.'

They suddenly went very quiet, and were clearly
creeping into the pavilion. Then all the lights came on,
flooding the room with illumination. Fortunately, we
observed that event from the road, having slipped down
through the changing room and out through a back window.
Upon reflection, I realised Anne had probably done that
before as well.

We ran across the road laughing, with the camaraderie
of having done something one shouldn't and got away with it,
and back towards the Tennis Court. It was quiet now; the
party had ended, and there was no sign of anyone. We got on
our cycles and headed along Grange Road past the rugby
ground. The street was deserted; we passed no-one, just the
ghostly white shape of a barn owl flapping by in search of
some vole in the margins of the playing fields stretching
behind the big houses. We turned up past the Anchor and
down Trumpington Street towards Addenbrookes. Despite her
earlier protestation, I could tell she liked the company as we
peddled on silently. Past Pembroke we met a few late-night
carousers, but no-one else till we reached the hostel. A quick
kiss and a wave and she went inside; just a whispered
farewell:

'Thanks, that was good and you were nice. See you at
the club.'

I cycled back towards the college, elated with that
pleasure that only getting away with eating forbidden fruit can

give you. As I passed the front gate I could see it was locked, so I cycled on down Trinity Street and turned off down Garret Hostel Lane intending to get round the back gate – not a difficult manoeuvre at the College, even with a bicycle. I flew over the deserted bridge and disappeared into the dark trees lining the Backs, following the narrow footpath with my front lamp. As I approached the College back gate I heard a murmur from the other side. Fearing it might be porters I turned off the light and hid in the darkness of the wood. The voices came nearer and I realised they were undergraduates, a man and a woman. Something kept me standing silent watching them. They were coming out of the college; the girl of course now well past visiting hours. They got around the gate easily and then I saw them clearly in the light of a streetlamp. It was Piers and Penny. Suddenly my taste of triumph turned to dust in my mouth…

At the end of Grange Road, just by the rugby ground, I made the familiar turn into West Road. Tennis Court Hostel lay on the left at the end and I turned into the drive. There was a mechanical ramp to prevent unauthorised use; otherwise it was as it had ever been. I parked and wandered down to the Hostel. I couldn't resist looking into my old room; it seemed amazingly the same. I crossed into the Fellows Garden. It was as well-tended and quiet as ever. Then I noticed a familiar figure sitting on a bench on the other side. He was dressed in open-necked shirt and canvas slacks, but even though it was thirty years on I recognised him immediately. I went over to him.

    'Hallo, Arthur.'

He turned towards me, a smile of recognition spreading across his face. 'I thought I recognised the voice. How are you, Stephen? Long time no see.'

He still had that rather innocent fresh look he'd had all those years ago, though now the rather boyish features were lined and the golden hair was grey.

'I'm fine, Arthur. Yes, it's been a long time.'

'Forty years. Just after graduation. I seem to remember seeing you in the distance outside the Senate House. I suppose we should have all met and said goodbye, however briefly, promised we'd keep in touch, even if we didn't mean it.'

'It didn't seem appropriate somehow, at the time. But when you're that age you think things will go on the same forever. I suppose I thought we'd meet up sometime, or bump into each other. But it never happened.'

'Not until today.'

'Have you seen...?'

'The others? Only Huw. I heard his voice booming out across Bradley's. You couldn't mistake that, could you? Exactly the same, just took me straight back.'

He got up, and I noted that his body, always slender, was now more sparse, and he moved like an old man. He noticed me looking.

'Had arthritis now for some time. Can barely play. But it doesn't seem such a loss as I'd imagined it would be. Come by car?'

'Yes, I'm parked just by the front of the Hostel.'

'Ah, that was where your room was, wasn't it? Mine was just behind. It all seems such a long time ago.'   He turned away, 'Must be getting back to the College. I've got my old room back in Bradley's. Reckon that's a mixed blessing. What about you?'

'I think I'm there as well. Haven't been across to the College yet.'

'Ah, well, mustn't keep you any longer. I'll see you when the festivities start. I think it's tea first.'

He shuffled off across the lawn, heading towards the gate out onto Queen's Road, across from the back entrance to the College. I watched him for a moment and then turned and went back to my car. Getting out my overnight bag I followed his path towards the College. The original metal gate out of the garden was like a portal into another world. Suddenly I was transformed from the world of forty years before into the modern day. The traffic down Queen's road was horrendous, and I was most appreciative of the crossing which temporarily halted it. Dodging the hordes of tourists, I made my way to the back gate, an elaborate affair in wrought iron with two side doors and a grand double entrance I had never seen unlocked. Each side was a water channel, and my mind went back to the nights when I had gingerly made my way round the outside, balancing precariously and glad when I avoided the drop into the unknown depths of the stagnant water below. And inevitably the sight of Piers and Penny... But today the side gate was open, albeit guarded by a college servant impressively attired in a purple edged gown, another innovation. I explained my business, and he allowed me to pass and proceed up the tree and stream lined path towards the bridge.

Nothing had changed. As I stood on the bridge leaning against the parapet where once we'd tried to catch the poles of unsuspecting punters, the panoply of the college lay before me. Across the huge back lawn lay Grange where that party had taken place so long ago. The end of the chapel next to it completed the iconic view seen so often in Cambridge backdrops, but which still had the power to overwhelm as it always had. I crossed the little humpback and descended towards the gravel path that ran besides Bradley's and Webb's and up to the curtain wall and round to the gatehouse with its octagonal tower whose four clocks were still telling the right time. The porters' lodge was pretty much as I remembered it, except for the ubiquitous computer screens, and the porters themselves seemed much politer, or perhaps that was a result of my age.

Having obtained my key, I made the journey back towards Bradley's. The literature had said we would have our old rooms back, and whilst I didn't recall the exact number, as soon as I reached the staircase I realised it was the same. Memories flowed back. Bradley's was a rather dour building on two sides of a courtyard, divided off from the path and tourists by a hedge. On the fourth side ran the river, with a little landing stage where the college punts were tied up. The staircase was dull and utilitarian, with the old blackboard bearing the names of its occupants in white still present. I climbed the stair and reached my old room. It was a strange sensation, like walking back into the past; it was as if the room had just been waiting for me to return. I opened the outer door, the 'oak' so often 'sported' in tales of Oxbridge and pushed open the flimsy green baize inner. The room was a set, that is a living room and bedroom, a splendid apartment more suited to the lifestyle of the rich young gentlemen of Edwardian England than the grammar school boys of the sixties, or the twenty-first century students for that matter. It was a privilege one only had in one's last year. It was the first time that I felt I was living like the gilded youth of that strange world before the First World War, so iconic that we all think we would have liked to experience it, forgetting it only applied to a tiny proportion of the populace. Before that the hostel rooms had been much more like the halls of residence at other universities that I later experienced on conferences. However, we had not had the staircase servants or 'gyps' in our day; that would I think have been too much for us in the Sixties though we still had 'bedders' as immortalised in Porterhouse Blue. Did they still exist, I wondered? Certainly the bed was nicely made up, with towel and soap laid out, a perk we had not received as undergraduates. I walked around the living room. Though the furniture was in a different style it was still basically the same: desk, bookshelves, armchairs, coffee table. The view from the bedroom looked out over the Cam, and was as stunning as ever. There was no bathroom, of course; we had always had to go down into the basement for ablutions. I undid my case, set out my evening clothes ready for the dinner, and then laid out on the bed. There was still an hour till the first meeting: tea in the Curwen Room, where that heated meeting had taken place so long ago. I closed my eyes and once again I was back forty years...

Chapter 8

The first time ever that she visited my room must have been in the autumn of that last year; I can still smell the wood-smoke and feel that chill that crept up from the river as winter approached. The nights were drawing in, and I had to light the lamp. She had read that J. R. Turner had spent a year in Bradley's and she wanted to see it. I didn't know which room it had been, but that late afternoon, standing by the window looking down on the dark torpid water, I could well believe that he had stood there himself. He was still in college then, up on A Staircase, behind a great pointed Victorian Gothic door off a corridor near the Hall gallery that towered above like a medieval cathedral.

She stood still, just looking out, her blonde hair falling straight over her shoulders; there was a faint whiff of perfume. I stood beside her, rather tongue tied, pleased she was there but embarrassed that I seemed to have nothing to say. She was dressed according to the uniform that many undergraduettes adopted: sweater and jeans, but with boots that cost a king's ransom, and a style that other girls could not dream of...

'It must be wonderful to be here, all the history and things. You are so lucky.'

I muttered some platitude; she turned and went to sit on the settee.

'New Hall is so... new! It's not like being in Cambridge at all. You men have all the decent colleges; we are in the afterthoughts.'

'I'm sure that will change sometime. We voted recently here to accept women.'

'But that will be too late for me.'

I made some tea and cut up some cake; we sat and ate and drank in silence. Then she spoke.

'Do you think everything else will be an anti-climax after this? Do you think we'll end up in dull offices or looking after squabbling children, and look back on these friendships, and our life, and wish we were back?'

'Maybe, but it is an unreal world, isn't it?'

She turned to me, her expression intense: 'But that's why we may never be able to match it. It's like Dorothy coming back from Oz. Nothing will ever be as intense or as much fun again. I'll even miss the pain. The red shoes will not be enough.'

She looked straight in my face: 'Do you want to sleep with me? I know you fancy me; I've always seen it in your eyes. I'm afraid I don't love you; it would just be sex. But then I don't love Piers either. I don't love anyone, never have. Perhaps I'm incapable of it.'

I could think of nothing to say. I don't think I was surprised or embarrassed; somehow anything that Penny said always seemed right for the moment. She just had that effect on me.

She stood up. 'I have to go now; I've got a supervision in an hour. Thanks for the tea, and showing me the room.' She came across and kissed me on the lips.

'If I didn't like you so much, I would sleep with you. But it wouldn't be fair. Though does that matter? There are no restraints here; we can do what we like. It will never be the same again. Don't bother to come to the door; I'll let myself out.'

She smiled and left. I sat for a long time, unable to move, listening to her feet pattering down the old wooden staircase, her perfume lingering mustily in the air...

The striking of the clock of Great Saint Mary's woke me with a start. I realised I had drifted off, and it was time to go down to tea. As I wandered in, I noticed most of the alumni were already in. There were to be about fifty of us, about half the year, not a bad turnout I suppose. I immediately recognised Huw, his lilting voice booming out over the room, as unchanged as Arthur had said. I had followed his career: trade union organiser and then Labour M.P. for one of the South Welsh valleys. He saw me straightaway and broke away from his conversation to greet me. He took me in a bear hug that owed more to the Noughties than the Sixties. A little too exuberant, covering the tension that was legacy of the last forty years.

'It's great to see you, Steve. Been far too long. I know why it was, but I'm glad you're here. Maybe we can finally put the past to bed, eh, boyo.' He appeared as self-assured as ever, but it didn't quite ring true. Nevertheless, anyone observing us would have thought we were picking up where we'd left off in college. I played the part as well, and we soon seemed to have dropped into our old ways. As we walked across to collect our tea he regaled me with the current political situation. 'It's right back to square one. We thought we'd beaten them, the toffs, didn't we? Set up a new world order. Now we've got an Old Etonian in Number Ten.

They've regrouped and even the Thatcherites, all those estate agents and shopkeepers that backed her, they've been outmanoeuvred too. It's the aristocracy back in charge, and we have to start all over again.'

I pointed out that we had moved on; social liberalism had triumphed, and economic neo-liberalism was in trouble. He smiled, 'Yes, there's still a lot to play for. What about you? How's life in your school?'

I expected him to accuse me of selling out, of betraying the movement by teaching in a public school, but he laughed it off.

'I'd rather have you teaching them than a dyed-in-the-wool Tory. You might even install a shred of doubt about where we're going. And anyway,' he said with a laugh, 'half our lot have their kids in private schools anyway.'

He still had that boyish enthusiasm, the conviction that what he was doing was right and worthwhile, even though there was now a touch of cynicism, even world-weariness. His face still had that young earnest look, but there were a few lines now, the jowls had grown and lengthened, the hair was thinner on top. Someone across the room caught his eye, and he touched my arm as he moved towards them.

'Must leave you now; someone I have to catch up with. Speak to you over dinner; I believe we are sitting together.'

He disappeared and I went across and collected a cup of tea and a cake. Turning away from the serving table I surveyed the room. It was a strange mix; the one common factor was our age. Some were formally attired in collar and tie, usually over a check suit or tweed jacket, the epitome of

Telegraph readers I felt. More were informally dressed like me in an open-necked shirt and casual jacket. A few were even in tee-shirt and jeans. A motley crew, as indeed we had been as undergraduates. I saw Torquil, now red-faced and portly, wearing a prominent silk handkerchief in his top pocket, talking to a rather arty fellow in a yellow cravat that I vaguely recognised as an ex-choral scholar who had appeared occasionally on the TV screen. I didn't go over. Suddenly I sensed someone at my shoulder; I turned and it was Piers.

'Hallo Stephen, long time no see.'

He had changed the most of all of us. His features were still recognisable, but his tall, willowy frame was now sparse and bent; there was a noticeable stoop. His blond hair was now grey, and thin, but still flopped over his forehead. But the things that hadn't changed were his eyes, still piercingly blue, and as alert as they ever had been.

'I heard you were a housemaster at St Breda's. That did surprise me; it's the last thing I thought you'd do.'

'It surprised me too. I suppose one just drifts into things, and then the mould's set.'

'Yes, I suppose so. Mind you, I never saw you as a revolutionary. I always thought of you as a bit of a fellow-traveller, if you don't mind me saying so. Huw could be very inspiring and persuasive; I wasn't surprised he ended up as an M.P.'

I just smiled. 'So, what about you, Piers? What have you been doing?'

'I drifted for a long while too. Whether it was guilt over what had happened, as I felt at the time, or just youthful rootlessness, I'm not sure now. As you know, I was always a bit of a dilettante, fancied myself as a poet, then tried writing lyrics, plays. Had the odd job in publishing, was driving my parents wild. But then I started writing seriously. I'm a professional writer, Stephen, now, and doing pretty well at it.'

'Really, I've not seen your name anywhere?'

'That's because I write under pseudonyms. I'm Arthur Sawbridge.'

Now it fell into place. I'd read some of the Sawbridge books, especially the Fenland Trilogy, and seen the films. I kicked myself metaphorically. I should have realised: the two names, the settings, how could I not have realised. It all made sense now: the atmospheric, psychological thrillers, the strange world of the Fens, the dark view of human nature that they all betrayed. Piers saw the glow of recognition and continued. 'I had to put down my thoughts and emotions, but I couldn't write a personal testimony; it was too painful. So I had to do it with fiction. I soon found I had a gift for it, both writing and storytelling; they're not the same of course. I didn't expect much from my first book, but it sold well, and it all blossomed from there.' He turned back to me. 'Sorry to use yours and Arthur's names; I suppose in a way I wanted to bring you in too. We were all to blame, weren't we, in one way or another.'

I looked away, unable to answer. The tea party was breaking up now.

'Next on the agenda is Evensong in the chapel. Are you coming?'

Another thing I had not done for years: voluntarily attend a religious service. Plenty of school prayers and services, but none for myself. Today it seemed finally right.

'Yes, I'm coming.'

'Arthur will be, of course. In fact, I believe he is playing the organ.'

I let Piers lead me out through the bar, where I noticed Huw was haranguing some of his old left-wing friends. I heard a snatch of it.

'Of course, for many of us New Labour was just a tactic; really our aims are the same as yours, but it's all to do with the art of the possible...'

He didn't notice me and I didn't attract his attention. We went out into the front quadrangle; the sun was setting now, and as it was late September an evening chill was just arising. We sauntered across the grass, gleefully ignoring the multi-language notices, enjoying the status and privilege we had not had as undergraduates. I wondered what the tourists, lined up to enjoy one of the must-see events in Cambridge, made of the elderly, all-male collection that now bypassed the queue and made our way into the chapel.

It was quiet, dark and cool. The great vaulted ceiling towered miles above. I remembered as an undergraduate being in a party taken up into the roof by an ancient history don, and being told some of the vaulting was only an eighth of an inch thick. Holding it up were the great Perpendicular pillars, adorned with the symbols of regal authority, the whole a paean to Tudor power and wealth. We processed through the screen and entered the choir where seats had been reserved for us, just behind the spaces to be occupied by the choir itself. As I sat down in the wooden pew, glancing at the order of service and other relevant religious tomes present, I couldn't but think of all those who had sat there before, trite I know, but true and sobering. Did the legacy that hung over me hang similarly over them? Perhaps, though perhaps a world in which all believed in forgiveness of sins and redemption was easier. For a second I envied them their certainty.

The singing was beautiful. I would have liked to say as beautiful as ever, but to my regret I never went much into the chapel. In fact, only twice I believe. It was a conscious decision; I was anti-religion at the time, and I regarded the whole business with the choir as old-fashioned and snobbish: the young choristers with their Eton suits and top hats, walking in formation behind the senior chorister. We would regularly see them, passing our Hostel from the adjacent choir school, across the road and into the South door of the chapel. Now I regret my prejudice against the traditional prevented me from hearing more of their sublime music. But we didn't do traditional in those days; I loved rock, folk music, the West Coast sound, the beauty of the antiphons and plainsongs lost on me.

I felt myself becoming maudlin in memory of wasted opportunity, and to focus my mind again I looked up at the huge stained-glass windows where the last of the sun was shining through. It was nearly time. Soon it would be the dinner, and we would all be together again, for the first time in forty years. My mind drifted back again…

During the days following my seeing Penny with Piers, I experienced a mixture of depression and anger. I was illogically furious with Piers, as if my unrequited and unstated desire for Penny should have precluded him from dating her. Equally irrationally I was angry with Penny for her imagined infidelity to me. But when the initial pain subsided, I resolved to ignore her. I spoke warmly to Piers when I next met him, and he responded, no doubt wondering what he had done previously to upset me. I avoided the two girls as much as possible, and concentrated on my work. It was deep into the term now; the autumn was a cold one and chill winds swept in from Siberia to bathe Cambridge each morning with a white dusting of frost. My homesickness returned as the Christmas vacation approached, and it was with a little relief that I said goodbye to my four friends and loaded my trunk into my father's car. The whole term had taken barely eight weeks.

However, though it is clichéd to say it, I was a changed person. Back home no longer felt like home; the identical streets of thirties semi-detached houses with their mock Tudor beams seemed so dull and phony against the glories of college architecture. I found having to fit back into family life irksome after the freedom of college life. I met up with old school friends of course, a couple of whom had returned from Oxford. We spent Christmas Eve getting drunk in a local pub, and nursed a headache through Christmas Day itself.

My return to Cambridge in January seemed like a release. I had felt increasingly claustrophobic in my London suburb, and my thoughts constantly turned to wondering what the other four might be doing. I imagined Piers enjoying a traditional Christmas on his family's estate, perhaps out hunting on Boxing Day (I had never seen Piers on a horse or heard him talking about riding, but it was just the thing I could imagine him doing). Arthur I could see playing the organ in some country church as the congregation heartily sang carols, and Huw down his local working man's club somewhere in the valleys inspiring an audience of miners with his revolutionary fervour. The only one whose life I couldn't imagine was Giles; perhaps I feared it might be too much like mine. I had left most of my things up in my college room, so I travelled back by train, taking the Underground to Liverpool Street, and then the train to Cambridge, a journey of just an hour and a half. I just had a small case with me, so it was no problem to catch the bus, and then walk from the bus stop to King's Parade. Even though this was only the second time I'd come up, it already felt like returning home. The Christmas decorations that had been up when I left were now of course gone, and it was a grey, bleak day, so I might have been excused for feeling depressed, but in fact I was elated, looking forward to seeing my friends again.

They did not disappoint; the joy and enthusiasm as we became reunited was genuine. Though we never discussed it, I think they felt the same disconnect with our lives back home. Soon we were back into our routine: lectures, practicals and late nights. I had almost forgotten Penny and Jo; my attempts to put them out of my mind having been largely successful, but at the first Chemistry practical there they were of course, Penny looking more beautiful than ever. However, it was Jo who came over.

'Happy New Year, Steve. It's good to see you again. We didn't see much of you at the end of last term, did we, Pen. Anyone would think you were avoiding us. Did you have a good Christmas? I thought about you during the hols, wondered what you were doing.'

The old routine was restored and we all ended up with beer and sandwiches in the Spread Eagle. As we were leaving Jo lingered behind; she obviously wanted to talk to me alone.

'There's a guest night in Hall on Friday. We can each bring a 'young man' to dine; it's a way the old spinsters on High Table try to make the college a bit less like a nunnery. Would you like to come as my guest, do say yes, it won't be a horrible as it sounds.'

Her face was a mixture of hope and apprehension. I could hardly refuse; I liked Jo, and wouldn't have wished to hurt her. It wasn't till much later that it occurred to me that she had shown the courage that I had failed to do with Penny. And in fact, invitations of this sort were much prized in female-starved male colleges. Then the implication set in; Penny would be there, and would Piers be with her? But I couldn't let such fears rule my life; in fact, it would be good to confront the situation; these things were always much worse in imagination than in reality. So on Friday I put on a collar and tie, not such unusual student wear then, and my only suit, and cycled out of central Cambridge and up the Huntingdon Road.

New Hall as the name suggests was one of the newest colleges, which when it was created increased the number of women's colleges by fifty percent. It had only been on its site for a couple of years and was housed in a typical sixties building, all concrete and glass, a dramatic contrast to the Gothic brick of the other two women's colleges, let alone the medieval men's ones. I nervously entered its portals and was directed to the JCR together with other male visitors, where a number of New Hallites were waiting in their best clothes for their guests. I saw Jo immediately, unusually wearing make-up, in what could best be described as a party dress, deep red with puffed sleeves and a cleavage, and very short even by the standards of the time. It suited her figure and perhaps for the first time I felt sexually attracted to her. Though she was no Mirabel Starr, the slight gypsy air about her added to her allure, as did the comparison with the other girls. In general, they were rather frumpish, a collection of blue-stockings. Inevitably I looked for Penny, and breathed a sigh of relief when I realised she wasn't there.

'Penny not coming to the dinner?' I asked guilelessly.

'No, she's got a party somewhere, much more exciting no doubt.'

I didn't of course ask with whom. The dinner was pleasant but unmemorable. Jo chatted throughout, and strangely I found her much easier to talk to than on other occasions. The absence of Penny seemed to have released both of us, and really we got on well. At the end, we started to file out towards the Porters' Lodge and I got ready to kiss her goodnight. But before I could do so she pulled me to one side.

'Here, round this corner.'

In a second we were into another corridor and out of sight of the rest of the diners. She gave me no time to argue or enquire.

'Quick, this way!'

We ran down the corridor and out through a door into the grounds. Jo led me through what seemed in the darkness to be an ornamental garden. We cut through flowerbeds and across lawns and finally ended up outside what was obviously an accommodation block. There was no noise; no lights seemed to be on in any of the rooms. We were by a fire door, obviously securely locked. Before I could ask her what was happening she produced a key from her handbag and opened the fire door.

'What on earth, how did you get that?'

'It's a skeleton key. Penny and I have one each: essential for getting in and out when we shouldn't, and getting people we shouldn't in and out too,' she said, winking. We went a few paces down a ground floor passageway till she stopped before a door that had a notice saying 'Penny and Jo' in large colourful letters. She opened the door and we slipped inside, Jo locking it from the inside.

'Won't you be in trouble if I'm found here?'

'You won't be.'

'What about Penny?'

'Oh, I don't think she'll be back tonight,' she giggled. I felt a sudden pang of jealousy but had little time to think about it. Jo led me to the bed which occupied much of the small bedsitting room. There was a desk and chair and a bookcase and wardrobe and that was about it. A star led up to a mezzanine floor on which was obviously Penny's bed. Jo turned off the main light and turned on the bedside light. In the half-light, we started kissing. I slipped my hand inside the top of her dress and she unbuttoned my shirt. The rest happened pretty rapidly. I remember struggling to unzip her bra, and her undoing my belt. Then suddenly she was standing naked before me. The curves of her body were accentuated by the shadows from the faint light and her dark hair hanging over her breasts and between her legs gave her an exotic appeal, like a Maya nude or a Renoir harem scene. She knelt astride me and put her hand over my mouth.

'Don't say anything; let me do it. Don't worry, I'm on the pill.'

I can still recall the feel of hot skin and her breasts against my chest. This time there were no interruptions. I don't remember much about it, but it must have gone better than the other time, judging by Jo's reaction.

'That was good; how was it for you, as the saying goes? Did the earth move?'

She was unabashed, confident, in charge. I realised later she must have planned it all. Also that she had probably done it before. What would have happened if Penny had been there? Fortunately, I thought of a, not terribly original, comeback.

'No, only the bed springs.'

She laughed, and sat up leaning on one elbow.

'Do you think I'm a tramp?'

'No, of course not.'

'Some would, not that I care. These are the sixties, sexual freedom thanks to the pill and all that. In fact, you're the first guy I've slept with at Cambridge. I'm very choosy who I sleep with.' She lay back with her hands behind her head. 'Choosier than you; you'd rather I was Penny, isn't that true?'

Her comment cut through any complacency I had felt. It was as if she could see into my soul. A cold sweat spread across me; my duplicity and hypocrisy was laid bare. She saw my discomfort and carried on: 'Oh, don't deny it; I've seen how you look at her, all doe-eyed. That's why I had to take the initiative. You'd have been happy drooling over her. You probably think she's virginal like a Pre-Raphaelite beauty, but believe me she's slept with more guys than me. Including one of your friends.'

'Piers.'

She sat up. 'You knew!'

'Yes, I saw them once coming out of The College.

She lay back, as if digesting the information. 'Well, I didn't know that.' Then she jumped to her feet.

'Get your clothes on. We'd better get you out of here. Can't have the bedders finding you in the morning.'

'Won't they notice Penny's not in?'

'Oh, I'll jump in her bed and throw a few clothes about. They think she's an early riser.'

Throwing on a dressing gown, she led me back through the door into the garden.

'Go across that lawn and over the wall and you're in Storey's Way. Go down past Churchill and you know the way from there.' She pulled me tight. 'I enjoyed that; I hope we do it again. Don't worry, you don't have to be in love; I'm not looking for a husband.' She kissed me hard and then ran back into the college. Within a minute her light was out, and I was standing in darkness, just the light of a half-moon to guide me across to the wall. I easily scaled it, and though I looked nervously around there was no-one. All was quiet; all was dark, just a lonely whoo-whoo of a distant owl. I walked back along Grange Road and up to the hostel. There were a couple of lights on, but not Piers'. Was Penny in there, I wondered? I knocked on one of the lit windows and its inhabitant came down to let me in.

'You must have had a good night.'

'Not bad.'

'Did you, you know, get your oats.'

I adopted a serious and sober demeanour: 'we're not all obsessed with sex, you know.' But back in my room I allowed myself a faint smile.

In the morning, the full implications of what had happened came home to me. I don't know about other people, but early in the morning, when barely awake, is the time that the reality of a situation played out the day before really hits me. I knew that what had happened in New Hall was going at least to affect the rest of my time at Cambridge. I was sure that Jocasta had planned the whole thing, but I could hardly claim I was tricked or misled. I had wanted to sleep with her, even if I had not considered all the implications. Or had I, really, in my subconscious, and gone ahead anyway. I liked Jo, and certainly had desired her last night. We were friends; we were going to be in close proximity regularly over our time in Cambridge. I had little doubt that Jo now thought of us as a couple, the carnal act sealing the commitment, like a medieval betrothal. And was that such a fate? Though I was still infatuated with Penny, I knew that she was unobtainable; it was a hopeless unrequited love. If she didn't exist, would I have been happy to have Jo? Quite possibly. If this was a romantic novel, I of course would have stayed true to my love, and it would all have come good in the end, but life doesn't work out like that. I thought of the advantages of a relationship with Jo, and listed them in my mind (rather unemotional, I know, but I've always been a list-maker, a balancer of the scales). Firstly, I liked Jo and she at least liked me. Secondly, she was no prude. Thirdly, in male-heavy Cambridge an undergraduate girlfriend brought prestige. And fourthly, I would avoid those end-of-party moments when the girl-less men are all gathered in the kitchen getting sadly drunk together.

So the decision was easy, but as the next lab session approached, and I would see Jo and Penny again, my nervousness and insecurity increased. What if Jo really didn't want a relationship, it had been a one-night-stand for her, and my decision-making was all in vain? After all, she knew about my desire for Penny. Was she the only one? Did anyone else know?

Chapter 9

A sudden sound of rustling and fidgeting brought my mind back to the present. The service had finished, and the tourists in the cheap seats were gathering their coats and bags together as the last of the choir filed slowly out. I put down the order of service and meekly followed the rest of the alumni back through the screen and across the huge nave, which more than ever reminded me of a railway station, and out into the open air, where the glare from the remains of the day made my eyes blink. It was still light and sunny outside, and on a whim I decided to stroll down to the river. The gravel path past the back lawn was busy: tourists taking pictures, academics carrying books and papers, local inhabitants using the college as a short cut, striding purposely about their unknown business. I ignored them all, and wandered down till I came level with the college landing stage. I cut into the small courtyard before Bradleys, and stood again looking down on the college punts, clearly identifiable with the purple paintwork, chained up side by side in the water. The river was busy, punts going in all directions, including broadside across the Cam. They were crowded with youngsters, there was much screaming and laughter and splashing…

It was our second year, the sophomore year as the Americans call it. My mood at the start of the new university year had been the opposite of mine the year before. Where I had been apprehensive, now I was confident. Where I had been uncertain, now I was assured. It only needed the presence of a new crop of freshers to make me feel like an old hand. This year I was given a room in the new building, the Crane Building, which now appeared, fully armed like Athena, from behind the builder's screens. The old court of Curwen reappeared, all turrets, ivy and Victorian gothic on one side, all glass, metal and concrete on the other. Now these sixties constructions are hated, but then it was the Gothic that was out of favour, and generally we welcomed the new brutalist architecture with its bare brick walls and huge ceiling high expanses of glass. A new kitchen and server meant we no longer ate formally in Hall. Cambridge was changing; gate hours were going; new buildings were springing up in all colleges and winning awards. And most significant of all, the spirit of 1968, of the soixante-huitards, was abroad in the university.

My room was on the third floor, if I remember correctly. The new building had corridors, not staircases, with the anonymity of any hall of residence, but we didn't care. We had expected to go into digs, and I had even visited a college house in Fen Causeway to meet the landlady, so finding myself suddenly in college, usually a privilege only afforded to finals year undergraduates, was a welcome surprise. The room was actually tiny, much smaller than my hostel room had been, the size of a hotel single room. That was no co-incidence, as I found out later these rooms had been designed with accommodating conferences in mind. At the end was a minute bathroom, no shower, but this en-suite facility seemed like the height of luxury, at a time when even decent hotels didn't have them. I would enjoy many an evening lying and reading in the bath; it at least gave me a break from the claustrophobia of the bed-sit. Sadly, it had no view, looking out over the roof of the kitchens: the worst view in Cambridge!

Since the night in New Hall it had been almost subliminally understood that Jo and I were what would now be described as an item. Jo was clearly happy with this arrangement, I more ambiguous. I still held a flame for Penny, but as she was going out with Piers my desire remained unrequited. We continued dating throughout the Michaelmas and Lent terms. I don't recall many individual instances; it all seemed to merge into one. Except for the punt party. By the time we got to the Easter Term, exams loomed. They were the last before Finals, and everyone started to take them seriously. For the first time, socialising came second. The cry 'sorry, I can't go for a drink; I must revise...' became a familiar refrain. I found revision quite hard myself for Cambridge exams, more than I had at school. It was as if now I was at Cambridge I'd made it, and I didn't see why I should have to prove myself all over again. I still assumed I would do well when I took my first-year exams: that results would come as easily as they had at school. Sadly, this attitude resulted in a poor second and an embarrassing interview with my director of studies. When I returned I resolved to do much better.

Those were radical times; there had been the Prague Spring, the student uprisings in Paris, the Vietnam demonstrations, but in Cambridge all was at peace. It was a hot summer, that second year, like the legendary one of 1914, great for lazing and reading by the river, playing tennis badly on the courts in front of Garden Hostel, and punting. Looking back, it was the last activity that set everything in motion. It started innocently enough. I had the idea of us all spending a day messing about on the river, punting up to Granchester to have tea like Rupert Brooke. It was a popular activity then, no doubt still is now, and would be a welcome break from our revision. I suggested it to the other four: Huw was involved in some political meeting, Arthur had a choir practice, so it was Piers, Giles and me. And of course, Penny and Jo were invited.

So that morning – it was probably a Saturday though I can't be sure – we all gathered at Bradley's Court. One side of the court ran alongside the Cam and there were moored the College punts. The College like other riverside colleges had its own collection of punts, six in total, attached to a small landing stage. We had booked one in advance, and it was the only one left. I fetched a pole and paddle from the store and Giles brought the cushions. The girls got into the boat with much squealing; it was a rare event. New Hall was the other side of town and had no such craft. They were obviously happy, and we all left the jetty in high spirits.

I punted first, standing on the raised platform at the end of the punt. These strange craft, originally designed for moving on the shallow waters of the fens, were shallow rectangular wooden boats with a hollowed-out prow, a raised stern and a central section where two rows of cushioned seats faced each other. The two girls sat next to each other, Piers lolled opposite them, and Giles sat in the prow. I'd had quite a bit of practice of punting by this time and had mastered the technique: drop the pole, which was about three metres long, vertically into the water till it hit the bottom, pull on the pole to propel the punt forward, and then lift it cleanly out of the water and into a vertical position to repeat the stroke. Once one had the punt going at a reasonable speed forward in a straight line it was actually quite easy.

We went past Queens', under the Mathematical Bridge, and then out into the basin by the Anchor pub, trying to avoid inexperienced tourists coming from the Scudamore boatyard. We navigated round to the slipway that took one up to the section of the river that led out of the city and towards Granchester. This section was higher than the part we were on, and ran through a weir to the lower by the Mill. As always in summer there were crowds milling around, many with drinks in their hands and yelling encouragement or derision at the punters passing by. The slipway had metal rollers, but was steep, and it took all our efforts to get the punt up the slope and launched on to the upper Cam. But soon we were on our way again, passing the Victorian buildings that were set back beyond lawns on both sides. We went under the road bridge at Fen Causeway and then we were clear of the city. Soon we were out in a flat pastoral landscape, nothing but meadows each side with tall grasses obscuring our view, so that we seemed isolated in our own universe. It was a hot May day, no breeze, and a perfectly clear blue sky out of which the sun shone unhindered. It was the first such day of summer, and we relaxed, the passengers almost somnolent in the centre of the punt. Slowly all conversation ceased, and we just took in the beauty of the day. There was virtually no noise, just the trilling of some larks high above, and the slow lap of the water against the bank as we passed. Looking back, it was an Edwardian scene, like those imagined from 1914. Piers in a striped blazer and straw boater, lolling like a young aristocrat, the two girls sitting demurely in sleeveless white blouses and long peasant skirts, Penny's long blonde hair almost falling into the stream. Giles in his prim long-sleeved white shirt and grey trousers knelt at the front, trailing his hand in the water. Piers had brought a picnic hamper – 'Just something I got the kitchens to make up for us' – and had tied a bottle of white wine on a string, which he hung over the side of the punt 'to cool it'. Miraculously, it survived this crude cooling system. With the picnic, we decided to find a spot to stop and moor to eat it. Such a spot occurred as we came around a bend. The river was wider there, and there was a kind of pool which the current did not enter. There was a piece of ground next to it where the undergrowth was low, and we could disembark. I steered the punt in and secured it by ramming the pole in to trap it against the bank. The girls got out and spread a tablecloth. Miraculously glasses and plates and cutlery appeared. The kitchens had done us proud: there were cold chicken, sandwiches, quiches, and of course strawberries and cream. The wine was uncorked with a pop that seemed to shatter the silence. We had long left any other punts behind, and so it was as if we were the only people in the world. It seemed a perfect day, and I knew it would stay in the memory.

'This used to be a bathing pool in the old days. Young men would come out here and swim, out of the view of any ladies.' Piers had sidled up to me. 'They wouldn't wear costumes of course.'

'Would anyone dare to do that now?'

'Why not? Come on, it's a hot day. I feel like a swim.' He began to strip off, and after a brief hesitation, so did I. Giles declined, looking embarrassed, and the girls turned away, pretending to be shocked, but not able to resist peeping. We both jumped in.

The cold took my breath away. The pool was deep, and I initially dipped under, for a second fearing my feet might get entangled in the weeds I could feel about them, but I bobbed up easily, and splashed about energetically to warm up. Piers likewise was swimming easily. We laughed and shouted to cover the effect of the freezing green water on our bodies. But after a few seconds it started to feel all right; I lay on my back, with the contrast of the hot sun on my chest and the icy depths below. The girls stood and watched, as did Giles. I tired of it first, and struck out for the side, pulling myself out. As the water droplets on my body evaporated I shivered uncontrollably, and Jo draped a wrap she'd brought about my shoulders.

'If you were going to do that you should have brought a towel. You'll catch your death of cold.'

The sun soon dried us, and we sat down half naked by the picnic, wolfing down a chicken leg whilst drinking a draught of wine. It would have been an incongruous party if someone had passed by: me with the wrap round my bare shoulders, Piers just in his blazer. Jo wrapped her arms around me.

'Poor lamb, you're still shivering.'

I looked across to the others. Piers was chatting to Penny, who seemed engrossed in what he was saying. I turned my attention to Giles, and was immediately disturbed by what I could see. He was looking at me and Jo, and there was clear anguish and jealousy in his face, no, not just that, hate and anger too. Then he saw me looking at him, and the expression went, and he reverted to his usually rather detached and dreamy air. It was as if I had imagined it, but I knew I hadn't. And I knew it was a look I shouldn't have seen. It sounds so trivial; how could a look have been so significant. But I knew it was. The mask had slipped and I'd been given a window into his soul, and what I saw was not just disturbing, but rather frightening.

The party continued, but the pleasure of the afternoon had deserted me. The others had noticed nothing, and chatted and joked as we punted home. Piers fell asleep, Penny lay back and looked like a Victorian painting. Giles sat silently as I punted. Though we said nothing, we both knew what had passed; the moment could not be undone...

Chapter 10

'Ah well, time to change for the bun fight.' It was Arthur again, hovering on my shoulder. 'At least we should get a good bottle of wine.'

I agreed with him on the excellence of the college cellar, and then hurried on ahead cutting across the little lawn towards the Bradley's staircase where my room was situated. It was a little rude to leave him behind but I just couldn't make small talk at that time. All sorts of memories were rushing about in my brain, which was acting like a kind of demented computer throwing out all sorts of jumbled thoughts into my imagination. I almost ran across the court and up the stairs, hurtling into my room and collapsing on the bed.

When I had calmed a little, I stripped off and pulled on a dressing gown. Forty years ago, I would have just gone down wrapped in a towel, but that seemed a little bohemian for a man of my advancing years, and of course there were women in the college now. But regardless of my attire, I saw no-one as I made my way down into the basement. The old bathroom with its huge bath was still there, and as I sank again into the deep cavernous white receptacle, feeling like a liner entering a dry dock, cut off from the rest of the world, a few of the demons rested from their labours and I got a degree of repose. I lay there till the water was cold and then returned to my room. It was getting dark now; the noisy punters had gone, and the water beneath ran silently past my window. A lonesome cow mooed somewhere in the meadow across the river; it could easily have been a rural scene, not the centre of a busy city. I started to dress for the dinner, my dinner jacket seeming a bit tighter than last time I put them on. I had found my old college bow tie, in college colours; it was still like new after decades locked away. I just about remembered how to tie it, and then looked in the mirror. Strangely, while dressing I still thought of myself as I had been the last time I'd dressed for a college occasion, but now seeing myself reflected I couldn't avoid the fact a middle-aged man stared back at me, not a twenty-something. Suddenly the memory of the first time I'd ever worn a DJ came flooding back to me…

At the end of our second year, Piers invited me to stay with him during the summer vacation. The invite came out of the blue; he had never invited anyone of us before, indeed, none of us had invited any others to stay either. It seems a little strange looking back on it now, but Cambridge always seemed something quite separate to the rest of our lives, as if our friends in college didn't really exist in the real world, and couldn't join us there. But just before we went down, as the quaint phrase goes, Piers tackled me one evening in the bar before hall. The others were not around. He drew me aside.

'If you're not otherwise occupied, would like to come and spend a few days at Pendlecombe. My parents are always asking me to bring some of my college friends home, and you are the person I'm closest to.'

I was touched and surprised by his invitation. Since the sighting of him and Penny, my feelings towards Piers had cooled, not something to be proud of, I know. But that was a while ago now, and things had effectively got back to almost what they had been before. But I did somewhat still concur with the Huw view that Piers was really a little ashamed of his 'plebeian' friends, and none of us would ever see the inside of his family seat. I stuttered my thanks and acceptance.

'That's fixed then. What about the end of June? The estate and garden look especially good then.'

Came the prescribed date, and I was alighting at a small station deep in rural Hampshire. It was almost a halt, and only two of us descended onto the platform. I felt myself going back in time as I walked towards the exit, with its wooden Victorian roof on ornate cast-iron supports, and banks of flower beds running out along the platform, behind the large faux-antique station sign. I could easily have imagined myself back at the turn of the last century, in a Sherlock Holmes adventure, my Dr Watson meeting Piers' Sherlock. But instead of the insistent 'choo' of the steam train as it pulled away, with that glorious smell of engine smoke making up for the bits of grit assailing one's eye, there was the mechanical noise and smell of the diesel two coach sprinter. Still, once it had departed silence fell on the station, just the faint buzzing of bees and a cow lowing somewhere o'er the lee. It was a beautiful day, still and warm, and my apprehension at what might be in store gave way to pleasure at the perfect scene. I was to be met, and in my current mood half-expected to see a pony and trap waiting for me. Instead there was Piers standing by a land-rover. He strode over and greeted me with a warm handshake.

'Delighted you could make it. Not too bad a journey, I hope. It's just a few minutes from here. Lot quicker than in the old days, eh.'

'I'm surprised this station wasn't closed by Beeching.'

'Ah well, that was down in part to my grandfather. He had a lot of influence with the government of the day. I think that swayed it.'

It was typical of Piers that he did not mention that his grandfather was both a peer of the realm and a cabinet minister then.

'In the old days, there were great weekend parties. The traps and carriages, and the only car, would be running relays to the station. It would be like Paddington. In those days, we had thirty odd servants, back before the First War. But all gone now. And good riddance, you'd say, with your political views no doubt. Huw certainly would.'

He drove now in silence, as we proceeded along quiet roads with the New Forest, one of the few remnants of the great forest that once covered all England, closing in on all sides. Then suddenly we were clear of the trees and in rolling countryside, all greens and yellows and browns, with plump white sheep and contented cows chewing away on the sward and ignoring us.

'This all used to belong to us.'

The sudden interjection surprised me. 'What happened to it?'

'Sold to settle death duties mainly, and debts. Some of my predecessors were very poor gamblers.'

After that brief dialogue, we were silent again until an ancient wall just set back from the road came into sight. I guessed it was the boundary of Pier's estate, but decided not to question him on it. It seemed to go on for miles, too high to be seen over, except by the mature trees I could see nestling behind it. Then a lodge came into view, next to a wide gate framed by two pillars with weather-beaten lions on top of them. Without a word Piers swung the car through them. We were then on a gravelled track which wound through some trees till suddenly a vista opened before us. Set back amongst open fields was a Georgian mansion, built of grey sandstone, three stories high with a pedimented and columned entrance in the middle; a platform with steps leading up from the front and the sides to an imposing oak door. In front of the house was a gravel semicircle with lawns around it. Piers without fuss pulled up and stopped right in front of the entrance.

'Welcome to Pendlecombe.'

My first impression was one of intimidation. I had never visited such a property except as a paying visitor to a National Trust property or the like. Coming as a guest was totally outside my realm of experience. I had no idea what to do once I had got out of the rover. I half expected a posse of black-and-white uniformed staff to pour out to welcome the 'young master'. But no-one appeared.

'Come on, let's go in.'

'Err, what about my case?'

'Oh, you can leave it in the car. George will collect it.'

So there were some servants left. George seemed such a suitable name; I could imagine an ancient retainer staggering out to take in the cases one by one. But before I could fanaticise any further Piers was bounding up the stairs and signalling me to follow him. He rapped on the door, and after a brief delay, it was opened by an elderly man dressed in a very old butler's uniform.

'Thank you, George, can you let mater and pater know I'm back with Mr Sawbridge. Bags in the Rover.'

George disappeared, and I had a chance to look around the hall. It was a light room, lit by a circular skylight at the top of the stairs, and by a large window below the entrance pediment. There were black and white tiles on the floor giving a chequered pattern, and a couple of landscape oils on the walls. The rest of the walls were covered with heads of antlered creatures, whose expressions seem to cast disapproval on my presence, and some ancient weapons: I recognised muskets, halberds and claymores amongst them. The staircase at the other end of the hall was magnificent. It seemed to hang in the air and wound up to the second floor, just below the skylight. There were portraits that I presumed were ancestors of Piers on the walls and the banisters and balustrades looked as if they were of marble. It was all very grand and imposing, though it was only later I realised there was nothing new or restored; the scene would probably have looked the same a hundred years before.

Piers led me into one of the rooms off the hall which was obviously the library; there were wall-to-ceiling bookcases on three sides of the room, with the other side having two huge windows looking out on to the front courtyard. I had always loved books, and still do, being as unable to pass a bookshop as a shopaholic might a department store. One of the first things I had done when I came to the College was to go into the library: all Victorian Gothic with bookcases to match that had probably been put in when the library was built. This library matched it in atmosphere, if not in size or quality of material. Looking closely at the shelves, it was obvious that many had not been moved let alone read in decades. Some were in a dodgy condition; there had clearly been some roof leaks over the years. In fact, there was still a small piece of damp in one corner of the ceiling, which I tried to avoid looking at, though inevitably my eyes were drawn to it.

'Can I leave you here for a moment, Stephen? There's something I need to take care of. Take a seat; have a look at the books.'

Having made that announcement, Piers disappeared. I looked around in surprise; I was sure he had not left through the door we came in. Was there some secret door behind the bookcases? It didn't take long to find; one section of books was false, and there was a door behind it. Presumably for the servants to come and go without being seen, I assumed, and it all added to the air of romance in the house. I expected Piers to come back shortly, but he didn't and I was left to occupy myself for some time. I tried some of the books, but didn't dare touch the oldest looking ones, all brown leather binding stamped in Latin in gold letters. I looked at some of the others that seemed less valuable and more sturdy, but they were not very interesting: ancient bound copies of Punch or the proceedings of local worthy societies. There were, amusingly, some modern whodunits, and I wondered who was reading those.

After a while, boredom drove me to the window. It looked out over the back lawn beyond a terrace framed with a low wall and stair frame by two pillars topped with a coat of arms each. In the distance, the fields and woods of the Wold spread out, and I wondered how far the estate now spread. Suddenly I saw Piers out on the terrace; he was in the company of a woman, who from her age and appearance I presumed was his mother. They seemed to be having a heated conversation, if not an argument. I couldn't hear what they were saying through the thick glass, and I didn't want to be caught watching them, so I returned to my seat by one of the bookcases, and engrossed myself in a 50-year-old copy of the Spectator.

'I'm sorry to have left you so long, Stephen. My parents would like to see you now. They're in the sitting room.'

Piers had reappeared as rapidly and invisibly as he left. He spoke almost as if I were being taken into a consulting room: 'the doctor will see you now'. I wanted to ask him about the secret door, where it led, but I was too overwhelmed by the occasion, and meekly followed him out, through the proper door this time. We crossed the austere hall into another room. This was a larger and more lived-in space. There were two tall windows again looking out over the terrace, and the ceiling was covered in mouldings of fruits and flowers that were clearly original. There was a large marble fireplace which was not lit, and above it a large landscape in oils which looked Flemish. There were other paintings on the walls, and some antique pieces of furniture that looked French, topped with pieces of porcelain, presumably Chinese, and were all clearly old and valuable. But these were the only formal aspects to the room. There was a modern coffee table, which had some magazines on it. I glanced at them; they included The Lady and Country Life – not my usual reading matter. But my glance around the room was brought to an abrupt halt when my eyes alighted on Piers' parents.

They were sitting apart, her on a chintzy sofa, he on a worn by comfortable armchair. Both were gaunt and austere, an older version of Piers, but with an authoritarian stiffness that could only come from an upbringing before the First War.

109

Neither rose, and indeed showed little sign of even seeing me. I felt like a junior footman on his first day. Not sure what I should do, I advanced towards Piers' father, holding out my hand.

'Good morning, sir, I'm Stephen Sawbridge. Delighted to meet you.'

He half rose, taking my hand with a limp grip, barely touching it in fact. He mumbled something, as if he could barely afford to expend any energy on me. I turned to Lady Pendlecombe. 'Delighted to meet you, ma'am.'

Like her husband, she remained seated, just offering a tight-skinned ivory hand towards me. But unlike Lord Pendlecombe, she turned her gaze towards me. Suddenly our eyes met, and I felt as if a bolt of lightning had struck me. Her eyes, unlike the pallid aged shell of the rest of her body, burnt with an intensity that was almost frightening. They were a clear blue, just tinged with the yellow of age, but with a fire undiminished, and I knew now who had created Piers and controlled his world.

'Sawbridge, eh? Is that the Chelmsford Sawbridges?'

'Er, no, I come from North London.'

'I knew a Sawbridge at Eton, back in '01.'

'No relation as far as I know, I'm afraid.'

'You're not one of Piers' Eton friends?'

'No, afraid not.'

They clammed up now, with a faint air of my having disappointed them. I was left standing, embarrassed in the centre of the room, neither having invited me to sit down. I don't know what I would have done next, but fortunately Piers entered at that moment.

'Would you like me to show you to your room, Steve?'

I readily assented, and took my leave of Lord and Lady Pendlecombe with relief. They now seemed to have totally forgotten about my presence, so I made a formal little bow to each as we left. As we crossed the hall, I realised Piers was laughing quietly to himself.

'What was that little bow at the end? You looked like a German footman.'

'I didn't know what else to do. Your parents are rather frightening.'

'Only if you let them. They have had generations of breeding to keep the rest of the common herd down.'

'But that hasn't affected you.'

'Only because I consciously prevent that from happening. Belief me, if I relax a moment, it comes out with an even greater intensity.'

He grinned at this point and I grinned back, though in truth I felt a little frightened still, of Piers as well as his parents. I was truly out of my comfort zone. We passed up the grand staircase, leaving on the first floor, and coming out onto a landing. High up in the ceiling was a large fanlight, which gave the only light onto the staircase. There was a selection of anonymous doors off the landing, the space between them interspersed with old prints and cartoons. Piers opened one of the anonymous doors.

'Here we are! We've put you in the Japanese room.'

It was not hard to work out why it was called the Japanese room. The wallpaper, which looked as if it hadn't been changed since the last century, consisted of red oriental dragons wriggling through a landscape of pagodas and river bridges, with kimono clad noblemen looking on. It was all red, green, yellow, violent colours even after all this time. I peered at the paper, and with a start realise it was hand-painted.

'Cost an absolute fortune when these wallpapers were put up. Can't afford to replace them now.'

The furniture looked just as old: a double bed, with a counterpane matching the furniture, a heavy oak wardrobe, a dressing table with a marble top, a bowl and ewer on it, an upright wooden chair.

'I'll leave you now to get settled in. George is bringing up your case. We dine early here, at seven, drinks in the lounge at 6.30. Oh, and we dress for dinner. Have you got a DJ with you?'

'No, I don't own one.'

'Never mind, I'll get you one of mine. We're pretty much the same size. George will bring it to you. He'll help you to dress.'

'I think I'm capable of doing that on my own.'

Piers laughed. 'I'm sure you are, Stephen, but you've not worn black tie before.'

'Black tie?'

'It's what people put on invitations. It means a dinner jacket with a black bowtie, as compared to 'White tie', which is evening dress with a white bowtie. In our family, family dinners are always in the former, whilst balls and other grand occasions are in the latter. Of course,' he said as he stood in the doorway, 'we're pretty old-fashioned, everyone used to dress for dinner before the war, even middle-class families, not just the decadent aristos like us. It will all be gone soon; the tradition will not outlive my parents.'

'You could keep it going, if you wanted to.'

'Well, that's a surprise, Stephen. I'd have expected you to want to see that kind of thing gone, in your modern world of socialist equality. But perhaps you think of us as museum pieces, a part of a forgotten world preserved for posterity.'

Before I could answer, he was gone. Almost immediately there came a quiet knock and George entered. 'I'll bring your evening wear presently, sir' he intoned as he put down my case. After he'd left, I went across to the window. It looked out over the back of the house, across the terrace and down over a vast lawn towards what looked like a lake. Beyond was a copse of oak trees and fields with sheep and cows in. A traditional English rural scene, unchanged for decades if not centuries. Difficult to match to the maelstrom of ideas and emotions flowing back in Cambridge. What would Huw make of it all, I wondered?

Chapter 11

Shortly George returned with Piers' evening wear. Despite my earlier comments, I was thankful for George's help in dressing, especially as I'd never tied a bowtie before. Piers had been right; the garments fitted as if they'd been made for me, which was a little surprising as I was a little broader and shorter. But then I made a strange discovery. As I put on the jacket, I noticed some initials written on the inside collar. J R S P. Surely not one of Piers. I looked more closely. It seemed little worn, but not new; not that old either. A brother's perhaps, rather than his father's hand-me-down. But why had I never heard of one. I was sure Piers said he was an only child. Still, that was something to consider later; now I had to apply my mind to the task ahead. I completed dressing, and at the requisite time I descended, dreading the reception ahead, but in fact it was better than I feared. His parents had invited over a couple of guests about our age, from the nearest manor, I imagined. We had a convivial meal, though the food was unexciting and not very warm. The latter fault was not helped by George serving all the food himself individually. Piers had briefed me on the way over as to table layouts etc, and I coped well with cutlery and glasses. My one faux pas came at the end of the main course, when inadvertently I gathered my plate with that of my neighbour, hoping no doubt to speed up the funereally slow meal.

'We do not stack!' resounded across the table from Lady Pendlecombe, and I crept back metaphorically into my hole. The meal finished, the ritual of the ladies withdrawing and the passing of the port commenced. I accepted a cigar from a humidor proffered by George, who then placed decanters of port and brandy on the table, and then withdrew in true retainer fashion.

'Well, young Sawbridge, Piers tells me you're a bit of a bolshie.' The comment from Lord Pendlecombe took me by surprise, as the conversation over the meal had been bland and uncontroversial.

'Well, I do believe that we need a more equal and fair society, yes, sir.'

'No doubt you'd like to see us murdered in our beds, or at least turfed out of our homes and estates.'

'No. not at all, sir, I don't believe in revolution, but gradual change to a better society.' I couldn't be sure if Lord Pendlecombe was serious, or just winding me up, having some fun at my expense. With that uncertainty, I batted the comments back as unemotionally and calmly as I could. As I did so, I caught Piers' expression. He was obviously enjoying my grilling, a small smile hovering round his mouth. Had he brought me here for this; was that the idea, to put the grammar-school boy in his place? But before the inquisition could develop any further, the other young man, a red-faced gentleman farmer whose only interests seemed to be hunting and women, piped up.

'What are the fillies like up at Cambridge, eh? Any good lookers about, or have they all got spectacles and braces.'

Piers turned to him with a withering look, and took a second or two to reply: 'You'd better ask Stephen that; he has more experience than I.'

'I thought you said you had a girlfriend, Piers.' I turned with surprise towards Lord Pendlecombe. I had assumed he probably had little or no interest in Piers' life at Cambridge, and certainly not his social life.

'Oh really, come on then Piers, what's her name?'

'Penny.' They all turned to me as I said it, flatly and singularly. Piers turned away with a slight smile on his lips, but one that told of disgust rather than humour.

'Why did you mention Penny?' After the post-dinner session broke up, Piers and I walked outside. We were standing on the terrace; it was still not perfectly dark, and bats and birds late to their roosts were circling above. Somewhere in the distance an owl hooted.

'I don't know; it just came out.'

'You quite like her, don't you? Oh, I know you're walking out with Jocasta, but it's easy to tell.'

The old-fashioned expression suited him and the moment. I said nothing.

'She'd be bad for you, you know that, don't you? I think she's bad for everyone.'

'But not for you?'

'Oh yes, for me too, but there's nothing to damage with me.'

There seemed no answer to that. We stood in silence for a moment, then Piers said, 'Let's walk down to the lake; it's lovely in the moonlight.'

He was right; the moon was just coming up, almost full, and with the not yet vanished twilight we could see nearly as if it were day. To get to the lake we descended across the huge back lawn, impressive, but not, I noted, kept as well cut as were the college lawns in Cambridge. As we neared the lake, its true size became apparent.

'My ancestors created this in the eighteenth century by damming the brook. That was the fashion then, Capability Brown and all that.'

The lake looked real enough to me, though when I looked closely I could see that there was a weir with a gate controlling the flow in. In looked badly rusted up, and like much of the house and grounds there seemed little maintenance. There were loads of rushes and other weeds choking it, though it was still impressive to someone who thought a back-garden pond impressive. We stood looking at the moonlight shining on the lake.

'Are there any fish in it?'

'Oh yes, it was stocked with trout years ago, and I think they're still there. We used to fish in it when we were children, but rarely caught anything.'

'We?'

'My brother and I.'

'J R S P?'

'Of course, the jacket. I should have told you, instead of pretending it was mine.'

'I didn't know you had a brother. You've never mentioned him.'

'No. He...died.'

'I'm sorry.'

'It was a long time ago. He was much older than me. My parents have never forgiven me.'

'Not forgiven you? Why?'

'For living when he was dead. That's why I can't be damaged. That's why Penny.'

'To protect the rest of male humanity?'

He turned and looked straight at me. 'To protect you, Steve. It's you she would destroy…'

There was a knock on the door. I opened it, and there was Huw, also dressed in a dinner suit, though with just a black bowtie.

'A bit pretentious, eh, boyo, that purple bow.'

'There was a time you would not have even worn a dinner jacket.'

'Yes, well, we mellow. Have to wear it nowadays for all sorts of functions. No cloth caps around now; we all have to be on message for New Labour.'

'I never imagined you'd become an M.P. Always thought of you as a firebrand.'

'Times, change, Steve. There's not going to be a revolution; at least in power the party can achieve some of the things we both wanted. Though you were always more pragmatic than me. But at least I wasn't as deluded as some.'

He slumped into a chair. The mannerisms were all the same, but like with me there was a weariness in his limbs. That youthful vitality had gone, but when he turned back towards me the eyes still had that fire in them.

'They think they've won, you know, the grandees, put us oiks back in our place. But we'll show 'em yet.'

I was ready now. Sensing the moment, he rose and straightened his tie. Then he came across and adjusted mine.

'Always liked to do it the right way, eh, boyo. Not a bad effort from scratch. I'm afraid I cheat with a clip-on. You just need a slight tightening, there.'

We left the room without speaking further, and headed up towards the Hall. The court lights were glowing now in the twilight, and there was almost a magical air as we walked past the ancient buildings, as if in a Disneyland set. As we walked together, for the first time in over forty years, another occasion came to mind when we'd gone together into an uncertain reception…

It was our first feast: to celebrate the Founders birthday. All we grammar school boys were apprehensive, not knowing what to expect, and feeling the public-school contingent had the advantage over us. Dress was lounge suit, though I noted some on the Plantagenet Society were dressed more exotically, in dinner suits, some of varied hues, and often elaborate bow ties, as if to show their superiority. If the idea was to intimidate us, then they probably were succeeding, not that we were about to show it. Everyone was present, even Huw and the left faction, Founder's Feast was a three-line whip. Anyway, it was a good feed, a much better menu than usual, and free good quality wine.

The five of us sat together; even Piers, who had eschewed the company of the Plantagenets, and, perhaps in deference to our attire, was also wearing a lounge suit. We were noisy and outspoken, determined not to outdone by the Plantagenets, who assembled on a nearby table. The high table filed in, the college servants started bringing round the starter and serving the wine.

It was several courses later that my memories kick in. I must have drunk quite a bit as I was feeling quite light-headed; we had also had some beer earlier which probably was not a good idea. But I felt quite high and happy, enjoying the scene and occasion that only an Oxbridge College can provide: the silver glinting, the candlelight illuminating the portraits round the hall, the choir trilling in the gallery. It was noisy and high spirited, but good-natured. Then suddenly a shout came from the Plantagenet table.

'Sconce, sconce.'

Sconsing was an archaic practice that had virtually disappeared from Cambridge; I heard afterwards that one hadn't been called in College in living memory. It's a challenge to anyone who dares to talk shop in a hall dinner. If the sconce is allowed by high table, the person challenged must either pay for drinks for all the challengers or drink from the sconce. If he drained the sconce, then the challenger must pay for it.

Of course, we didn't know that at the time, and we were totally perplexed as to what was going on. Then someone explained. Huw was supposed to have mentioned his subject in some conversation; I've no idea what it was. Looking back, I'm sure some of the Plantagenets, probably including Tarquil, had planned it from the beginning. One of the Plantagenets got up and walked towards high table to ask permission for the sconce, but before he got there Huw got up and spoke out to the silent hall.

'Don't worry, bring the sconce, boyo, I accept the challenge. Bring it here.'

There was loud cheering and banging of tables. After a short delay, a parade of college servants brought in the sconce, held high, whilst the undergraduates stood and clapped the entrance. The sconce was a large silver tankard, probably holding a couple of pints. The college servants placed it on the table in front of Huw, and two of then opened bottles of beer and poured then in, filling it to the brim. Huw climbed up on to the table, having loosened his tie, and we passed the sconce up to him. We watched as the first half went down quite easily, and then it got slower. The sconce was almost horizontal, and some beer, probably fortunately, was running out the sides. But then suddenly he was draining the last dregs and placing the sconce upside down on his head. Pandemonium broke out. Everyone was cheering and shouting, we were slapping him on the back and gesturing at the Plantagenets. Some of them were understandably annoyed, and things looked like they could get out of hand. But then the President of the Plantagenets rose, and, walking over to Huw, offered his hand. Huw, perhaps surprisingly, shook it warmly. Cheers all round, and excited chatter across the room at an incident that would go down in College history.

As he regained his seat, Huw laughed off my congratulations. 'It was nothing, Steve bach. We have similar challenges in the clubs in the valleys. A couple of pints is no problem.'

'Maybe things are not so different after all.'

He looked at me quizzically but said nothing. I remember no more of the dinner, except at the end the sconce had taken its toll. Giles and I had to help Huw to bed, and left him snoring very drunkenly as we staggered off to our own rooms…

We joined others filtering into the Senior Common Room for our pre-dinner drinks. Arthur and Piers were there already, and the four of us were drawn together as if by magnetism. We stood in a little cluster, waiting for one to break the ice. Piers spoke first.

'So, what remains of the Famous Five are reformed. I didn't expect that ever to happen.'

'Don't get carried away, Piers. This is a one-off.'

Piers turned to Huw. 'I know that. But as with the mating of rhinos, it's amazing it happens at all.'

Piers' joke broke the ice, and we all visibly relaxed. A waitress appeared at my shoulder with a tray of drinks.

'I think the toast must be 'Absent friends',' I ventured.

'No, that's too negative. 'The Famous Five'!' Piers put the accent on the last word, and we all nodded silently and raised our glasses.

'Well, look who's here. We didn't expect to see you here. Thought you all hated this sort of thing. Especially you, Huw, tradition and all that.' It was Torquil, looking even more self-satisfied than he had been as an undergraduate, and decidedly fatter. His face looked bloated and red-cheeked, and his manner even more unctuous.

'I've no problem with tradition, boyo. Only with those pompous bastards that exploit it to line their own nests.'

I looked sharply at Huw, fearing his comments might cause a scene, but Torquil just smiled, as if his barb had achieved the desired result.

'Well, I can see I'm not welcome here. Enjoy the dinner. Hope to see you on future occasions when you decide to grace us with your collective presence.'

Suddenly a gong sounded. All conversation ceased. 'Would you please take your places in the Hall, gentlemen.'

The call to dine moved us all out of the SCR, through a corridor I had not been in before, lined with pen drawings of past fellows, some of which I remembered. We shuffled into the Hall itself. The sight was magnificent, with candlelight picking out the college silver spread out on the tables. Up above, the beamed roof disappeared into the darkness, and the ghostly portraits of past masters loomed out of the shadowy walls. Up in the gallery, the choir sat in their starched white surplices, ready to serenade the diners. We found our table, where we four occupied one end, with an ancient fellow at the end itself. Our places were marked, but next to us was one unmarked. As we all stood nervously, waiting for the High Table occupants to enter, no-one came to fill it. My attention went back to the imminent ritual. I recalled immediately such parades in my day. Then there had been a distinguished array: Doggart, the old emeritus Master stomping in with his heavy tread, and the peerless J. R. Turner, a tall gaunt figure, slightly stooped and needing assistance, a living legend there as part of the fairy-tale. The current selection was no match: the current Master, an American lawyer, with the member of our year who was to reply of behalf of the guests, a journalist from one of the broadsheets.

Once grace had been said, and we were all seated, I realised the empty seat had still not been taken. As the waiters came round with the first wine, I asked about it.

'It's been set for a late addition to the dinner, sir. We didn't have time to produce a name tag.'

'Who is it; do you know? Why isn't he here?'

'I'm afraid not, sir. He did apparently say he might be late.

The meal unfurled as the choir sang, and the ancient fellow wittered on, clearly unable to remember any of us. I remembered him from the party in Gibbs. Then he had been witty, snobbish, sharp and dismissive; now he was an old man struggling to recall the past. I humoured him, and we even found a few common acquaintances to talk about. But gradually we ran out of reminiscences, the conversation faltered and ended, and he turned to talk to Arthur about chapel life in the 60s. Those on each side of me were now engaged in conversations away from me, so I had a moment to enjoy my own thoughts and the occasion. The empty seat was still empty; whoever was going to occupy it was obviously not coming. I wondered idly who it might have been, but with nothing to go on turned my attention to the progress of the dinner. I looked around at the pageant in front of me. All of us in black tie, the candles, the silver on the table, good food, the waiters serving wine from the college's own cellar, the choir singing in the gallery. We were the revolutionary generation, in the most left-wing college in Cambridge, the children of the sixties, the ones who were going to change the world, or at least Cambridge…

For my last year I was to be in Bradley's, generally considered the best rooms in the college. I went from being in the newest building, a typical 60s confection of concrete glass and metal, into a building which, though in fact built in the early 20th century, was in the tradition of Cambridge accommodation going back centuries, all separate staircases, rooms clustered round a landing, like it had been in the Middle Ages. Now I had room to spread out, a relief after the constrictions of my sophomore room. Despite its size, I had entertained Jo there on a few occasions. Our relationship had been somewhat tempestuous. I often thought of the relationship between Hugh Walpole's Francis Herries and Mirabel at the time. I didn't love Jo, and she knew it. She said she didn't love me and it didn't matter, but I think she lied on both counts. We would row angrily, usually over Penny, who still was going out with Piers, though not very exclusively. Sometimes Penny would deliberately flirt with me; not that that was anything special, she flirted with everyone. I always felt, though my desire for her was as strong as ever, that my love for her would always be unrequited; her real attention was turned towards those with the greatest prestige in undergraduate circles: the famous actors, Union Presidents, that sort of thing. So I would even after the most violent of arguments, usually accompanied by floods of tears, streams of obscenities and the throwing of hairbrushes, return and makeup, and she would gracefully accept. And, it had to be admitted, we were reasonably compatible, interested in politics and folk music, keen to explore the area on our bikes. So my second year ended with us still as an 'item' to use that dreadful twenty-first century word.

Settling in at the start of the final year was fun. We were now the senior undergraduates, the top dogs, and could look down on the years below with a condescending eye. A major reason for this was the accommodation. Bradley's was

125

very different to the rest of the college. Built at the start of the twentieth century in a restrained Gothic style, it joined to the Victorian Gothic masterpiece of Benet's and ran down to the river. Half-enclosing a small court cut off from the main drag through the College by a small hedge, the fourth side was the river itself, with a little landing stage for punts from where we set out on our Granchester expedition. The accommodation was archetypal traditional Cambridge, with undergraduates having 'sets', not rooms, with the famous 'oak' to sport on the outside and the green baize door leading on to the living space with a bedroom beyond. Views through mullioned windows completed the fantasy, looking out over the Cam as if from castle walls over a moat. An environment that none of us would probably live in again. No wonder these sets were much treasured, but I was fortunate to get one high up overlooking the river. The practicalities though, once one actually started to live there were not so romantic. The bedrooms were unheated, the only form of warmth being a gas fire in the living room. All toilets and bathrooms were in the basement, a long way to go in the middle of a cold winter's night. The sets were situated on a staircase, with steep stairs which I could go up and down a lot faster in those days. There was a kitchen or gyp room on each landing though. The equipment was primitive, gas rings and kettles though there was a tiny fridge. A Spartan and inconvenient way of life: we all loved it.

I had barely arrived on my return for the next year when Huw knocked upon the door and poked his head in. he didn't stand on ceremony and entered and sat on the sofa before I could offer a word.

'It's going to happen, boyo, right here. Here, of all places.'

His face glowed. I sat down in a chair opposite. 'What's going to happen?'

'An occupation, Steve bach. Just like at LSE.'

He made it sound like the storming of the Winter Palace. I suppressed a smile.

'So what's the reason for it? What will be the justification?'

'To show that things are changing, boyo. To show solidarity with students and workers standing up for their rights everywhere. The old structures are finished. We'll have a university based on the principals of socialism, run by a progressive alliance of students and teachers. The medieval world of the dons and professors will be swept away. As the workers take control of their factories, we will control our colleges. It will be a new world, boyo, this is our chance.'

I resisted the temptation to say nonsense. It was clear that a summer spent back in the valleys with his Trotskyite friends had fired him up and instilled a revolutionary fervour. It must have been like that in St Petersburg in 1917. Did he really believe it; did they really believe it back then. Sometimes it happened, true, but now in Britain did not seem the time. But there was a febrile atmosphere around the university, it was true. As if everyone was waiting for something to happen. It was a year for revolutionaries, of course, if not actually for revolutions. The Sorbonne and LSE had already seen student occupations. But Cambridge, despite a sizeable far-left element, seemed an unlikely venue. It was overwhelmingly apathetic, there were no Tariq Alis or Danny

Cohn-Bendits. But I didn't want to upset Huw, so I humoured him.

'How do you know about all this?'

'Look you, there are plans afoot, mark my words. There are many people who share our ideas, in all colleges.'

Huw had assumed I was as committed as he for a couple of terms. He had finally persuaded me to join the Socialist Society, though my attendance owed more to a desire to stop him pestering me than any political enthusiasm on my part. I have to say I was not impressed. The meetings were interminable, with many motions and amendments and points of order. A lot of the business was about affairs abroad, showing solidarity with foreign trade unionists, and the like. All well and good, but I couldn't really believe a miner in Chile, say, would be much impressed by fraternal greetings from a society in Cambridge. Or perhaps they would? Who could really tell?

After Huw had left, I sat and thought on what he had said. He really believed, of course, and the milieu in which we lived encouraged it. The College was a hot bed of student insurrection in those days. There were always posters on the college notice board advocating one cause or another to support, and all the left wing political flavours had their own society and clique.

'Why don't you come to the meeting tonight? As privileged students, we have a duty to stand up for those who don't have the opportunity.'

'The system's rotten; it's no good trying to reform it. We must destroy it root and branch if we are to build a better world. And it's up to us to lead.'

Much of it sounds like nonsense now; I think it did then, but Huw had a way of carrying you along with him. Seeing the musical 'Les Misérables' years later, I could recognise Huw there: the hopeless revolutionary who dies on the barricade. But sixties Cambridge was not nineteenth century Paris; none of us gave our lives for the cause. Unable to concentrate, I abandoned unpacking and wandered down to the bar. Piers was sitting there drinking a glass of wine. Unusual at that time, I noticed he would often have one when on his own, but always drank beer with us. I collected my usual pint from the long bar and joined him in one of the little alcoves with its weird green light shade above. The bar was already starting to look a shade worn; modern materials were not showing the resilience of the medieval fabric.

'Huw's convinced the revolution is upon us.'

'Well, if they want someone to lead waving a huge red flag, I'm sure he'll be their man.'

'Seriously though, he suggested there were plans to do an LSE.'

'An occupation, you mean? Yes, I'd heard something like that. So, would you be involved in such an enterprise?'

'No, of course not.'

'I thought not; you're much too sensible.'

'You've never had much time for Huw, have you?'

'Oh, come now, I've never said that. In fact, I find him amusing, in his own inimitable and probably unintentional way. I'm afraid I can't take him seriously.'

I finished my pint and left him getting stuck into a second glass of Burgundy. I wanted to wander across to New Hall, see if Jo was back yet. In these days of mobile phones, ascertaining such information is easy, but in those days communication, if not quite as restricted as in Jane Austin's day, was still difficult. Though I was still not in love with her, and more certain than ever of that, I found I was missing her. I hadn't seen much of her over the long vacation, just a hurried meeting in London when she'd been staying with her sister, and we'd toured the British Museum and walked through Regent's Park together. I'd spent most of July and August back-packing round Greece and Turkey; the beauties of Ephesus and the Parthenon crowding out thoughts of Penny and Jo. Now as the familiarity of life in Cambridge gathered round me like a well-loved coat, I found myself looking forward to seeing her again.

As I collected my bike and spun out on to King's Parade, up Trinity Street and towards Castle Hill, I looked around at people going about their business in the usual way. A more unlikely site for a revolution I couldn't imagine. It was an Indian summer, a late flurry of wind-still autumnal sun that made living in Cambridge such a pleasure. As I pedalled furiously towards New Hall, I realised that this was the last autumn I'd see at Cambridge. Soon I'd have to start making plans, think where I was going, get a job. This sudden realisation almost pulled me up short, but I cycled on and pushed it into the back of my mind. There was still a whole year to enjoy, a year when we were the top dogs, those who knew the ropes, the ones with the experience. We should be able to avoid the mistakes of our first two years, but would that just make room for others?

When I reached New Hall Jo wasn't there, but Penny was. Strangely, this took me by surprise, as I thought for some reason she wouldn't arrive until the last moment, that arriving early wouldn't be cool. But there she was looking as good as ever in tight jeans and a pristine white blouse, her blonde hair hanging loose across her shoulders. She greeted me with the usual mixture of camaraderie and detached nonchalance; one minute I was her bosom friend, the next the man who'd come to read the meter.

'Jo not back yet?' I said with a lack of originality.

She shrugged. 'I expect she'll be here soon. Do you want to wait?'

One part of me wanted to stay there gazing at her; the other wanted to leave and stop torturing myself with unrequited desire. To prevaricate, I mentioned that I'd just left Piers in the bar. If she was surprised he hadn't come over to see her she hid it well.

'Is he in good spirits?'

'Yes, I think so, if ever Piers can be truly in good spirits.'

She smiled at that. 'Piers is a sweetie, but he can be very intense.'

'I think he cares a lot for you.'

'Does he, I wonder? Anyway, is that wise. Should we love too much? Doesn't that make us vulnerable?' She got up and started to unpack one of her cases. I thought that a good point to make my excuses and leave. She smiled and waved from her bedroom, and I knew her mind was far away now. As I left I had a sudden involuntary surge of joy, at the thought that maybe her relationship with Piers was fading, followed by the depression of thinking that probably she already had some luminary in mind, even if she was not already flirting with him. Gossip had already come to us that she was not exactly faithful to Piers, though we through friendship kept them from him as much as possible. Wanting to clear my head I jumped on my bike and cycled away down the towpath of the Cam. Despite the warmth of the day there were few people about, and no boats on the water. The air was hot for October and still, and as I cycled inches from the slow-moving black river the sweat started to pour off me. I stopped at the riverside Pike and Eel, and drank a pint from the wood in two or three draughts. Then I cycled on, till I was out in the fens, the flat landscape devoid of houses, and nothing but the river to keep me company. I turned off from the towpath and found a spot where I could lie out with my bike on the ground beside me. I lay back resting my head on my hands. I closed my eyes, and was almost asleep when suddenly I sensed someone approaching on a bike. Sitting up, I realised it was Giles.

'Sorry, Steve, I hope you don't mind me following you. I needed to talk to you.'

He laid his bike next to mine and then knelt down beside me. I was a little aggrieved that he had followed and violated my solitude, though I realised it would probably have led to a maudlin bout of self-pity. However, looking at his manner, I recognised a pent-up anxiety in him that I had seen before, but which seemed strange at this point in the term.

'You O.K? Is something wrong?'

'There's always something wrong. It's this place, Cambridge I mean. It's so phoney, not the real world. We all pretend it's so important, so stimulating, but the real struggles are going on elsewhere.'

'Vietnam, do you mean?'

He turned to me with a look that was a mixture of exasperation and pitying. 'I'm not just talking about wars, it's the whole of society. The whole unjust edifice. Poverty and oppression whilst we argue about what the Plantagenet Society get up to.'

I was inclined to agree with that. I'd heard enough tortuously circular arguments about things we could not influence to last a lifetime. 'I know what you mean, but any individual has very little influence on their own. All we can do is support those who best meet our aspirations, who want a better and fairer world.'

He threw himself back on the grass. 'I'm disappointed in you, Steve. I thought you had more fight in you. The politicians will never change society, especially not those on the left. They just want to posture, to feather their own nests. Direct action is the only course that will work. We have to at least frighten the Establishment; that's the only way anything will change at all.'

'Well, I think you have something there.' We grew silent; no-one spoke for what seemed like ages. I lay back, the warm sun on my face as I watched some fluffy clouds slowly slide across my vision. All was peace. Eventually Giles spoke again.

'You are lucky having Jo, you know.'

Immediately I remembered the look on the Granchester. Something in my face must have given me away, because he turned and stared straight into my eyes. Fortunately, he misinterpreted the look.

'Yes, you are, very lucky.' Then came the bombshell.

'Oh, I know you really would prefer Penny,' and then, seeing my look of horror at his comment, 'I see it in your eyes; a lovelorn expression as you gaze on our Zuleika Dobson. Don't worry, I won't tell her.'

I didn't know what to say. Of course, I could have denied it, but that seemed futile. I could have added that she already knew, or suspected, but I didn't, of course. We drifted into an uncomfortable silence again. Then Giles piped up again.

'Has Huw told you about the occupation plans?'

I sat up. 'Has he been talking to you about them?'

'Yes, we need to show our solidarity with other students and show we've got the guts to resist.' He grabbed my arm in a sudden burst of excitement. 'If there's an occupation here, at the heart of the Establishment, think of the effect it will have. They will have to sit up and take note.'

I was worried by Giles' show of enthusiasm. Huw being committed to such an enterprise was one thing; he was quite capable of looking after himself, but Giles was a different matter. He was too vulnerable, too naïve for such a course of action.

'Look, Giles, you must be careful. You could be rusticated for involvement in such a venture, or even arrested. What would your parents say? And even if it happens, which I very much doubt, what will it achieve? Do you think sitting in some university office is going to bring the revolution? It won't. Have some sense.'

He turned away angrily. 'You're the same as all fellow-travellers. You pretend to be a progressive, but really you're quite happy with the status quo. You're either too complacent or too cowardly to stand up for what you believe in.'

That was too much. I stood up and glowered down on him.

'That's enough, Giles. I will always stand up for what I believe in, but I'm not taking part in futile gestures that will achieve nothing, and I hope you'll do the same.'

There was little more to say. Giles picked his bike and without a word started to push it back towards Cambridge. After a few strides he jumped on it and pedalled away without looking back. Letting out a sigh I wearily followed him. After a hundred yards or so I drew level and we cycled wordless side by side back to The College. As we dismounted to lock up our bikes he turned to me.

'Still friends I hope, Steve?'

'Of course.'

'Good, I value your friendship. I'm sorry if I offended you out there. Sometimes I get carried away; I speak without thinking.'

I put my arm around his shoulder. 'It's OK. No offence taken. A lot of what you said is right, but we are not Che Guevaras.'

He laughed at that, and we went back into the college together. Giles went into the Porters' Lodge and I continued alone. As I crossed the Front Court, Huw came hurrying up to us.

'I must speak to you. It's urgent.'

I went to his room. As soon as we were inside, he closed both doors, after looking around to make sure no-one was around. As I showed my amusement at his behaviour, he put his finger on his lips.

'Got to be careful, boyo. Walls have ears; careless talk costs lives.'

I laughed at the string of clichés, but my mirth froze as I realised he was in deadly earnest.

135

'If even a whisper gets out, we're done for. There are reactionaries even in The College who'd go straight to the Proctors if they knew.'

'Knew what Huw? What are you talking about?'

'The occupation, of course. It's definitely on, and soon.' He stopped for a moment, and then continued, in such a tone that I knew something important was coming.

'The question is, Stevie, when the time comes will you be with us or not. Will you have the balls?'

I laughed. 'This is not storming the Winter Palace. You are not building barricades against an army. It probably won't even be very heroic. If it goes off at half cock you could end up being rusticated for nothing.'

Huw didn't hide his frustration. 'That's the trouble with all you so-called moderates. You spend so much time sitting on the fence you could be torn in two down the perforation. I know you want the same as the rest of us; you hate the system as much as me, but you'll do nothing to change it.'

'There are democratic ways of changing things, without committing a possible criminal offence.'

He laughed. 'There's no law in this country against trespass. We don't intend to damage anything, just make a protest.'

I wasn't convinced. The temptation to look for documents and other evidence of 'selling out to the establishment' would prove irresistible to many, and I knew there were some nutters who would definitely cause damage, and others with even darker motives. But I was stung by Huw's implied accusation of cowardice. Though I still was sure the occupation was a bad idea I equivocated.

'Well, maybe you're right. In any case probably nothing will come of it.'

For a few seconds, we sat silently. Then as if on cue there came a knock on the door, and in came Giles.

Huw turned to him. 'Steve and I were just discussing some very interesting developments, weren't we, Steve?'

As I didn't reply, he went on. 'We were discussing really striking a blow for the people here, of actually doing something, not just talking about it.'

Giles turned to me, and to my surprise I saw he was more animated than I'd ever seen him.

'We've got to do it, Steve. It's the only way. They pay no attention otherwise; it's only direct action that has ever achieved anything. Think of the French Revolution.'

'I don't see the likelihood of guillotines on Parker's Piece.'

'Don't be flippant; it's only an example. Do you remember the battle with the Plantagenet Society? Have they moderated their behaviour? No, they are as arrogant and overbearing as ever.'

He did have a point. The Society had continued their meetings after a brief break, and still trashed the JCR and vomited all over the quad, though it seemed less so than in the past, and they certainly kept well clear of the Lefties. However, I couldn't see how occupying the Old Schools would stop that.

'You're too…' he stuttered for a bit and then continued 'civilised. Urbane, moderate, taking the middle path. That gets nowhere, Steve, you've got to stand up for what you believe in. Make a stand.'

Huw jumped up at this point, more excited than I'd ever seen him. 'Yes, boyo, yes!' He grabbed him warmly by the hand. 'It's great to have you with us, Giles. I must admit I'd sometimes thought you weren't really committed to the cause, but now I know you are.' The two, shoulder to shoulder turned towards me. 'Come on, Steve. You're either for us or against us. Which side are you taking? That of the people or of privilege?'

What could I say? 'With you, of course, Huw. You know that.'

He hugged me warmly, and the three of us mutually joined hands. It was an emotional moment, and even I, still really far from convinced, was caught up in the excitement of the moment.

'Well, boyo, I must leave you now. Got a few more people to see.' He made it sound as if he was going straight to the barricades. Images from Les Misérables came into my head; the omen wasn't good. I didn't expect them to meet muskets, but proctors and police were a distinct possibility as was a swift departure from Cambridge. As the two of them departed, I went across to make myself a coffee, shaking my head as I thought back over our conversation. Whatever way I looked at it, it was a hair-brained idea. But then perhaps like many plans spun in college it would all come to naught.

But I was wrong. When I arrived at Lensfield Road for the next practical, there were little huddles of students in the entrance hall, with much animated and in some cases angry exchanges. I saw Penny and Jo, and crossed to them.

'What's happened? Why's everyone so het up?'

'Haven't you heard? They've occupied Old Schools.'

138

Old Schools, in the medieval court next to the College Chapel, were the university offices. So Huw was right. Was he already there?

'When did this happen?'

'This morning. There are already television and press there. What do you think? Are they right.'

I didn't answer Jo's question immediately. Whilst I was trying to frame a reply, one came from someone just behind me.

'It's a disgrace; who do they think they are? I'll bet it's grammar school commies, no respect for tradition.'

I turned around. It was a face I barely recognised; he worked on a bench some distance from me. I didn't think I had ever spoken to him, let alone known what his political views were. But I knew now.

'I think actually there is a long history of students rebelling against the authorities, going back to the Middle Ages' I retorted, without much actual evidence to back my view. But I didn't want to engage in debate with him; there was a much greater concern. Normally Giles was one of the earliest at practical sessions, always there before me. Today there was no sign of him. Remembering what he had said that day in my room, I feared the worst. I saw another College man who knew Giles, and pushed my way across, to him, grabbing him by the shoulder as he was just about to go up to the labs.

'Mike, have you seen Giles today?'

He turned to me in surprise. 'Didn't you know? He's taking part in this occupation. With Huw. I saw both of them in the crowd outside the Old Schools.'

I thanked him, and, as the throng pressed on up to the labs to start the practical session, I stood still and let them go. Then I turned on my heel and left the department. There was no doubt in my mind; I had to go in myself. I couldn't leave Giles alone in there; God knows what he'd get up to. Huw I wasn't worried about; he'd always end up ok, but Giles? I cycled speedily back to College and dumped my books and then walked the short distance to the Old Schools.

The Old Schools, as they were known, were situated next to the College Chapel, but predated it, being completed at the start of the 15th century. They had originally been the Divinity and Law School of the university, hence the name, and situated on a busy road, but when Henry the Sixth started to build his eponymous college, the road was cut off, and the buildings isolated, dwarfed by the huge chapel rising behind them. The College itself took them over and Old Schools was part of the College till the nineteenth century. Now it was back with the university, but as offices. Tucked away in a cul-de-sac that lead nowhere, it wasn't perhaps the best place for a high-profile occupation, though the other end did look out towards King's Parade.

I entered through the imposing medieval gateway, thinking that it would not have been difficult to close it against all comers if someone inside had the foresight. I crossed the court, little changed when Henry must have first stood here and dreamed of his great college, his gift to future generations. Though it didn't quite work out the way he expected, I think he would be pleased with how things have turned out, a better memorial for him than the dreadful roll-call of Wars of the Roses' battles and his lonely and brutal end in the Tower. But once those fleeting thoughts had passed, I headed into the building itself. There were lots of students milling around, all trying to look like Tariq Ali. I have an old photograph taken then still in my study, my one claim to a revolutionary past. Everyone looks far too respectable, some even wearing ties and sports jackets. Someone is operating a Gestetner, the cutting edge of communication technology then. The photograph was taken in the Council Room, under a huge portrait of a Tudor worthy, wearing almost comical pantaloons and staring down disapprovingly on the disrespect of modern youth. But that scene came later. First, I wanted to find Giles. I went from room to room, asking those I recognised (the College was well-represented here) if they had seen him. At last I found him, sitting in a corner, wide-eyed, absorbed by the whole pageant. He looked at me, and I was disturbed by what I saw; it was as if he were in a trance.

'I knew you'd come, Steve. I knew you wouldn't miss this; you wouldn't let us down.'

I could see it was hopeless to try and persuade him to leave, and I couldn't abandon him. So I just smiled. 'When did you get here?'

'I was with the first ones in. It was so easy, I thought there'd be some resistance, but we just walked in and occupied the building.'

I was tempted to say it wasn't exactly the storming of the Winter Palace, and there had always been access to the Old Schools: libraries and lecture rooms were there apart from the offices. But he went on:

'You see, when we stand up to the Establishment they crumble. There is nothing to fear but fear itself.'

I didn't think that FDR's words were entirely apposite, and displacing a few puzzled dons and clerks hardly constituted routing the Establishment, but he was so pumped up, and, yes, actually happy, that I couldn't comment further. In any case, I never had the opportunity. Suddenly a blow descended on my shoulders and a familiar voice boomed in my ear.

'Great to see you, boyo, knew you'd come, knew you'd stand with us.'

It was Huw, of course, but a different Huw. He seemed to have grown, a taller, more imposing figure somehow, even his voice was louder and deeper. Is this how demagogues are made, I wondered, people who believe their time has come? Cometh the moment, cometh the man? I wasn't sure what to say to him, but it didn't matter, he had moved on. I decided to wonder around and see what was happening. As usual, when you get a group of political enthusiasts, not to say fanatics, together in such a small space and under such conditions, all sorts of opinions, ideas, diatribes were floating around the smoke-filled air. No-one could agree on anything, of course, and there was no real leadership, despite Huw's valiant efforts. Banners were prepared and hung out at the end of the building, where large windows looked out above the loggia at ground level towards King's Parade and the Senate House on the left. The College chapel on the right completed an enclosure of a tidily cut lawn with railings at the end cutting it off from the Parade. As I looked out I could see already some bystanders gathering. There seemed no sign of any attempt to dislodge us, and I guessed there wouldn't be, not yet anyway. It wasn't Cambridge's style; they would try and ignore us as long as possible. I smiled to myself as I went back into the building. It was a long time since such an uprising had occurred in Cambridge. Our medieval forebears would understand it much better than our 20th Century ancestors. Scuffles with town louts and with the police on Bonfire Night, the Bertie Wooster japes of the upper classes were all that had occurred in recent decades. Not that the gathering around me was exactly working class; the accents that rebounded spoke of education in expensive schools, no matter how their owners tried to hide it. But there was an element now, typified by Huw and Giles, which was new. But I knew there was still a gulf between us and those town inhabitants looking at us through the railings. They would still think it was students playing, nothing to do with them, and frankly they would be right.

As might have been expected with us unworldly students, no-one had made any proper preparations. There was no food or sleeping arrangements organised. Someone had some sandwiches, and someone else some chocolate. But we were all too attuned to college-provided meals, as though the inhabitants of Animal Farm found themselves after their revolution unable to feed themselves. Some fanatics seemed not to need any sustenance; their revolutionary zeal driving them on to run up broadsheets and pamphlets seemingly the only manna they required. Of course, there was some booze; Huw surreptitiously extracted a couple of bottles from his bag.

'Here, boyo, get this down your neck before the rest of the thirsty bastards see us.'

The warm brown ale was very welcome, but did not make up for the lack of food, or the fact I spent a most uncomfortable and cold night trying to sleep on a window

143

seat. But I don't remember wishing I prepared properly, brought a sleeping bag. That would have been too much like approving the whole venture, and I had every intention of getting Giles out the next morning.

But we were still there the next evening, or was it a night later? I don't recall clearly now. All I do remember was the last evening. That is engraved in my memory like a photograph on an old plate, that even as my memories fade comes clearly to mind whenever something, a word or view or a sound, triggers the response. It was a crisp and cold evening, a harbinger of winter, there may even have been snow on the ground. The atmosphere was febrile; there was something electric in the air. I know it's a cliché, but that describes it. All day there were rumours of attempts to remove us by the authorities. I think some of the hotheads would have liked that; they could have claimed police brutality or state oppression, even though the coppers in those days would have been in their usually helmets and uniform, not dressed up like starship troopers as they are now for such occasions. But to the disappointment of many, nothing happened. Not till it got dark. Then a bizarre scene erupted. From nowhere the area around the Senate House was filled with right-wing hearties. Some kind of organisation had taken place because they clearly came from a number of colleges. Many were in evening dress, all had been drinking, all had that raucous arrogant air that so irritated us grammar-school boys. If anything were likely to turn me into a revolutionary Marxist, that display would have done. But in fact, I just thought how pathetic it all was, the extremists on both sides rivalling each other in their anger and hatred. Then it all became silly. Someone started blowing a hunting horn,

singing of Rule Britannia broke out, or maybe it was another
patriotic song. In retaliation, the traditional anthem of the
Left rang out from inside the Old Schools:

The people's flag is deepest red,
It shrouded oft our martyred dead,
And ere their limbs grew stiff and cold,
Their hearts' blood dyed its ev'ry fold.

Then raise the scarlet standard high.
Within its shade we'll live and die,
Though cowards flinch and traitors sneer,
We'll keep the red flag flying here.

Even I joined in; it was a time for taking sides and
there was no doubt then which side I was on, even if only by
default. We sang it, clenched fists raised, as if we were facing
the bayonets, not a few drunken Hooray Henries. Tempers
were stretched, the temperature was rising; I felt it only
needed one trigger to set things off. Then I saw Giles. He
had slipped away from the windows over the lawn where most
of us were glued. Then he suddenly was at my side, and in
his hands was a fire extinguisher. He turned to me with a
queer look on his face.
'This will cool them down, Steve; this will put out
their fire.'
He got the extinguisher up to the open window before
we reacted.
'No, don't be stupid! Grab it someone!' It didn't
take much to get the appliance off him. Was he really going

to do it? What would have happened if he sprayed the crowd?
Fortunately, we never found that out. I now kept a tight watch
on Giles, and after that frisson of excitement, the evening
progressed as before. Bystanders started drifting away.
Someone called the fire brigade who turned, ladders and all,
adding an increasingly surrealistic note to proceedings.

The standoff lasted most of the evening, with the mob
outside threatening to remove us by force, and restrained from
doing so by the policemen and Proctors present,
inconveniently for the extremists inside. What would have
happened had the two sides not been separated? Would there
have been a massive punch-up? Somehow I doubt it, but
many of the occupiers played up the threat in days following
and later.

'Oh yes, boyos, they wanted to frighten us out, but we
stood firm, boys, we stood firm.' Huw's proud refrain was
repeated ad nauseam in the coming weeks.

The final denouement ended in a typical British
compromise. What it was exactly I don't recall, but it resulted
in us all filing out of the Old Schools, running the gauntlet of
the mob outside. There were shouts of anger and derision on
both sides, and some spitting, I regret to say, but eventually
we were out and clear. The occupiers and hearties dispersed
into the night. The whole episode seemed like a dream; we
were back in the familiar Cambridge streets, all was as ever,
there was no revolution. Huw, I and a carefully supervised
Giles made our way back to College. Everything was just as
it had been when we left; the porters bade us good evening as
we entered. We ended up in Huw's room, talking long into
the night, too adrenaline-filled to sleep despite the lack of it
the night before.

Chapter 12

It seemed I had only just turned out the light and rested my
head on the pillow as I returned from my evening ride, when a
vigorous knocking broke into my sleep.

'Come on, you lazy bastard. The bus will be waiting
for us.'

It was Huw. It took me a second or two to figure out
what he meant, and then I remembered. I had agreed to go
down to London with him and many other students to lobby
Parliament about the size of the grant. It was the Easter Term
after the occupation. Following that incident, the political
scene in the university had gone very quiet, as if the
confrontation between left and right outside the Senate House
had caused both sides to draw back. The next evening after
the evacuation, Piers had joined me as I sat in the college bar.

'Enjoy your occupation?'

'No, I only went there to watch over Giles.'

'Ah, your brother's keeper. Can he not be trusted to
look after himself?'

'I worry about him. There is an unworldliness there;
he's easily swayed. I was afraid he'd do something stupid,'
and I narrated the episode with the fire extinguisher. Piers
grew a thin smile.

'Ah, I see what you mean. And what about the
college's answer to Che Guevara?'

'You mean Huw? He reacted much as expected,
railing against the forces of reaction.'

Piers was silent for a while, then turned to me, and I
was surprised to see a grin across his face. 'It's all rather

amusing, the posturing on both sides. It's impossible to take any of it seriously.'

'Were you in the crowd outside?'

'Yes, but just on the periphery. I kept well away from Tarquin and his chums. I didn't stay long. Too many that I knew were there. I've seen their unpleasantness before; I didn't want to witness it again.'

The way he spoke those words made me think there was a personal experience behind them. 'Is that why you aren't very friendly with some of your schoolmates?'

But he refused to answer, changing the subject, and I let it go. I had long felt there was a bad experience at school in the background, but I could never get him to talk about it. One by-product of the occupation, though, was that Huw now regarded both Giles and I as fully paid-up revolutionaries.

'You must both come down to the Soc Soc', the Socialist Society for the uninitiated. After much earlier pestering, and mendacious promises to attend the next meeting, I had been occasionally. It was as bad as I expected, middle-class Trotskyites planning the revolution amongst the proletariat, a breed as remote to them as Chinamen. I agreed to go again, tolerated a couple of meetings, then even Huw realised my heart wasn't in it. Strangely, Giles refused from the start to attend.

'It's just posturing, Huw. If you really want to change things, you must become a worker yourself.'

For all his revolutionary zeal, that was clearly not a prospect that appealed to Huw. Even then, he was looking towards an academic career. I think he could see himself as a left-wing lecturer or eventually professor, at some redbrick, much the sort of character Malcolm Bradbury created. I still didn't know what I wanted to do, but politics was certainly not it. It started to worry me a little as the final year progressed. My parents were pestering me to make up my mind, and I knew when we came back for our last term some decisions would have to be made, which seemed too mundane compared to our uprising. Looking back now, it seems almost Ruritanian, an irrelevant gesture divorced from real lives, but in the closeted world of Cambridge it looked quite different at the time.

When the new term surfaced, political interest grew again, though this time in a more practical direction, likely to get more support. It must seem odd to anyone today that we should be aggrieved despite having our tuition fees paid and a living allowance on top, but that's human nature I guess. Did we really care that much? I think I was more interested in a cheap day out in London, perhaps most of us were. But definitely not Huw. He really believed still. Fortunately for our friendship, my lack of revolutionary zeal did not affect his opinion of me. My involvement in the occupation had cemented that. We were Old Schools veterans, and as so revered by the left. I suppose, on a bigger scale, those who stormed the Winter Palace were regarded similarly in Russia. So my ambiguous and rather flippant attitude to the demo did not bother him too much.

Usually I enjoyed a coach trip, but that day the scenery, admittedly mainly the flatlands of Cambridgeshire and Essex, held little attraction. I spent most of the journey staring unseeingly out of the window. Even the chanting and slogan shouting from the far-left enthusiasts barely penetrated my consciousness. The bus took us right through London to Parliament Square. I remember little of what we did there. I seem to think there were some banners, and some protesting on the pavement, and some of us got inside the Palace of Westminster, quite legally I should add, and filled in forms to summon our MPs to speak to us. I remember a couple of us talking to one, maybe he was mine, I can't remember now. I do recall he spoke to us in the way we have now become accustomed to in programmes like Question Time: placatory, sympathetic, committing to nothing. As far as I recall nothing came of our visit, or similar ones: perhaps that explains what came later.

After the political business had been done, we had the rest of the day in London ahead of us. The coach wasn't leaving till later that evening. Unsure what to do, we went into a pub nearby. I was sitting with a pint next to Huw, who was still haranguing me on the necessity for further direct action, and Giles, who was saying little, when Piers appeared.

'What on earth are you doing here, Piers? I can't believe you were on the protest.'

Piers just tapped his nose.

'Quite right, my boy, but the Jacobins needed a bit more finance for their revolution, namely,' he smiled, 'some more bodies on the coach. And I was ready to oblige. Up the revolution.'

He brushed aside our ideas for the evening. 'I know a club in Soho; I'm a member, where we can have a good night. Lots of girls; it'll be an education for you.'

We must have all agreed to go to Pier's club, because that's where we ended up. It was just off Old Compton Street, in a dingy alley whose only other occupants seemed to be dustbins. The doors were all shut, with nothing to say where they led to, except for one. It opened into a plain brick wall, but there was a single lit sign above it saying in red letters 'The Playmate Club', with a line drawing of a scantily dressed woman to indicate exactly what kind of playmate was suggested. The door was firmly locked, but Piers knocked; a small window opened, and after a quick conversation, the door opened and we were admitted.

The door led to a steep flight of stairs in a corridor lined with red flock wallpaper, a bit like an old-fashioned theatre. At the bottom, we turned sharp left past a small cloakroom in which a very bored and fat man sat reading the Daily Sketch. Piers passed some money across to him and he motioned us into a large room which was half lit and very smoky. It was crowded with an amazing crowd of inhabitants, many of whom seemed to be foreign, but with a total mix of classes. Voices that sounded as if they came from barons intermingled with voices from barrow-boys, plus more than one conversation in a language I couldn't understand. Some were dressed in suits, some in colourful attire that certainly wasn't seen then outside London. There was one thing most had in common though; they were almost all male, generally middle-aged and well-heeled. There was no shortage of money; I saw customers passing large notes across the counter at the bar. Judging by that, the drinks were exorbitantly expensive, certainly by our student standards. We felt very young and out of our depth.

'It'll cost the earth to get a drink here,' Huw whispered to me. 'Why did we let him persuade us to come? We should get out of here.'

I was inclined to agree; like Huw, I felt ill at ease. Having been brought up to think that Soho was the ultimate den of iniquity, I knew I shouldn't stay. But another side of me was fascinated by it, a subculture that was so different to life at home or in Cambridge. So I said nothing, just looked around. The little bar covered one side wall, whilst at the end of the room there was a small stage. It was only a foot higher than the floor and tables pressed right up against it. The seats next to it were clearly the most prized, as these were full of the most affluent looking customers. A small combo of guitar, sax and drums sat on one side of it and were playing some pretty good jazz, though nobody seemed to be listening.

'Why are we here? Whose stupid idea was this?' There was dissention in the air in our little party.

But that didn't worry Piers: 'what are you having, lads?'

'We can't afford the drinks here,' I started to say, but Huw broke in.

'I'll have a pint of bitter, Piers,' and then to my embarrassed and condemnatory look 'well, he's got the money and it was his idea, wasn't it?'

We all with varying degrees of reluctance ordered beer. Piers strode up to the bar, greeting the barman as if he were his brother. Meanwhile we managed to find a table in a corner. It was rickety, and the stained cloth hadn't been changed recently, but we were all very happy to disappear into the dark depths of the club; our presence masked by the smoky and dimly lit atmosphere. In a moment or two the beers appeared and we sat in silence, drinking slowly, none of us wishing to be the next to buy a round. This was not a problem at the next table where a noisy party was drinking something that looked like champagne. There were two fat old guys; at least they seemed old to us though they probably wouldn't have been much more than forty. They were both dressed in flashy suits that didn't really fit them, and they wore so much gold that they might have come straight from a strike in the Klondike. The one nearest to me had a couple of huge rings on his right hand, which he was waving airily at the girl sat next to him. She was wearing a short thin silk dress that made little attempt to hide the curve of her body. She had blonde, obviously dyed, hair down to her shoulders, and heavy makeup, which she added to, at least with regard to her bright red lipstick, every couple of minutes. She was chain smoking, discarding the half-smoked butts every few minutes into the heavy glass ashtray at the centre of the table. Each butt was liberally endowed with her lipstick, necessitating the regular topping up process. I found myself entranced by this ritual and the whole image at the table; suddenly this scene changed from the sordid and exploitatory to an exotic example of the demimonde, as if we were in Paris at the fin du siècle, in the Folies, or the Moulin Rouge. Looking back just after at the time I felt the comparison trite, but now the world of Soho in the sixties does generate just that image.

'Do you think they are gangsters, and gangsters' molls?' Giles was obviously also swept up by the exotic nature of the club.

'No, just rich exploiters, with their whores,' said Huw unsympathetically.

Prostitutes, that had not occurred to me, but looking again I saw his point. It was not likely the men had brought their wives with them. I looked again; I had never seen a prostitute in the flesh before, they weren't readily seen in the respectable London suburb where I was brought up, though I suppose that they must have been around somewhere. But my musings were interrupted by a roll on the drums. We turned our attention to the stage. A bright spotlight came up, and out from behind a curtain came a woman in a long evening gown. She was made up much like the woman next to me: dyed blonde hair almost down to her waist, almost mask like makeup dominated by the same very bright carmine lipstick. There was a microphone on a stand at the front of the stage, and she started to sing into it: a song popular in the fifties, but accompanied by gestures that Vera Lynn or Alma Cogan would not have used.

Then, without warning, she stopped singing and started undressing. First, she started to remove her long, old-fashioned gloves, peeling them off slowly, but too slowly for some punters who encouraged her to 'Get on with it'. She reached out to one of the punters at the front and let them pull them off, and then she broke away coquettishly and turned her back, unzipping her dress. Immediately I thought of nights before with Jocasta, and felt myself turning red. She wriggled out of her dress; underneath she had on a black lace bra and suspender belt with a red G-string below. We sat motionless, scared to move in case we interrupted the performance. She had just got to the point where she was wearing only the G-string when there was a sudden commotion on my left. Giles had jumped to his feet. I looked at him; his face was red and his fists clenched.

'Stop it, stop it now.'

Even as he stood I could see bouncers moving towards him. While I was still taking in the situation he turned to me.

'This is disgusting. We shouldn't be here.'

Before any of us could move he was on his way to the door, evading the bouncers and pushing men out the way, oblivious to their angry comments. Like a guided missile he could not be turned from his course and he soon disappeared through the crowd. One might think this would cause a big disturbance in the club, but the very moment Giles left, the stripper removed the last vestige of clothing. Giles' dramatic act was swallowed up in the raucous reception; even his hurried departure was masked as the punters pressed forward for a better view.

'Come on, we better go find him,' said Huw, who left in pursuit. I got up to go but felt a hand on my arm.

'Let them go, Stephen. We've got something better to do.' Piers grabbed my arm and led me towards a door beside the stage. It was empty now, and the band was playing again. The customers were on the move too, some to the bar, others filling positions at the front vacated at the end of the show.

'Come on, this way.'

We passed through the door and into a passage which ran beside the stage. At the end was another door on the left and we went inside. There was a dark narrow corridor with doors off. As we walked along it one opened and an exotic dancer, all feathered head-dress and spangled underwear came out. She didn't even acknowledge us; just pushed past.

'In here.'

We entered one of the doors. It was obviously a dressing room: costumes were hanging on racks; there was a long mirror over a shelf with naked lamp bulbs all round it. Sticks of makeup were scattered in front of the mirror. The room smelt of sweat and perfume intermixed with cigarette smoke; it was airless, claustrophobic and very exotic. I was stunned and immediately apprehensive; this was not the kind of place a sober natural science student expected to find himself in. But Piers was obviously at home.

'Come and meet Jennie, Stephen; she's just been on the stage.'

I turned to see the girl who had just been stripping. Up close, the heaviness of her make-up and the dye in her hair was obvious and overpowering. She seemed quite old to me then, but was probably about thirty. She was still naked as when she had just left the stage, but was now wrapped in a dressing gown, a violently red coloured one covered in yellow dragons. Together with the heavy atmosphere, the intense light and the multifarious items scattered about the room, the effect was to make me feel confused and sick. I pulled myself together and held out my hand. 'Pleased to meet you, Jennie.'

She had a cigarette hanging from her mouth. Without removing it she took my hand and replied.

'Hi, pleased to meet you, Stephen. Hope you liked the show.' With that she turned away.

'I need to take a shower. I'm finished for the night.' Without any embarrassment, she dropped the robe and stepped naked into the open makeshift shower at the end of the dressing room. Strangely, her nakedness now was much more shocking to me than it had been on stage a few moments before. But I couldn't take my eyes off her. Her body was not perfect, but it was still alluring, and I had seen very few naked women, and certainly not so close up. Piers meanwhile was pouring us two glasses of what looked from the bottle like champagne. He saw my face and smiled. 'Oh, it's not real champagne, just a cheap fizzy wine, but it's free to us; punters are paying a fortune for it out there.'

He was quite right. Even to my untutored lips the fizzy liquid was nothing like Champagne, but I drank it all the same, rather revelling in the naughtiness of it all. 'Shouldn't we be drinking this out a shoe?' I giggled to him. Piers affected a weary smile.

'We're hardly in Edwardian England.' Then, seeming to be bored by the situation, he grabbed my arm again. 'Come on, I've something more exciting lined up. We're going to a party.'

'A party, what kind?'

He smiled: 'not the kind you get in Cambridge.' Shouting out, 'See you later' as we departed, he pushed me along the dinghy corridor again and up a metallic circular stair. At the top, he pushed open a door and we were outside again, but in a different alley to the one we'd come in through. We wound our way through a maze of back alleys and yards, all looking much the same to me, and all in almost total darkness except for the odd streetlight perched high up casting a poor illumination on the scene. But after what seemed like walking for miles, but was really only a few hundred yards, we stopped outside a closed door. It was set in a large house that once had been an imposing dwelling but was now hemmed in by a higgledy-piggledy collection of later buildings, and had clearly come down in the world. The windows were grimy and shuttered, and no light came from any of them.

'This is the place, Stephen.'

'What place, where on earth are we?'

Piers made no reply, but like a magician produced a key from his pocket and opened the black, opaque entrance. Inside, there was actually some light, though not much. We went down a short corridor and up a staircase in front of us. The walls were not dully painted, as I expected, but covered in a red flock wallpaper, with prints at intervals. I glanced at the prints, and then, doing a double-take, looked at them again. They were erotic studies of naked women, and couples engaging in all sorts of lewd behaviour. Suddenly I felt a shiver of apprehension: this couldn't be what I thought it was, could it? The next few moments are jumbled in my memory, my fear of the situation driving out my appreciation of the scene. We were briefly introduced to people, male and female, passed through several rooms, had a drink shoved in my hand. Clearly everything had been arranged in advance. Then suddenly I was in a room on my own with a young woman. The door closed and I was standing there looking at her. For a few seconds no-one spoke, the girl, for she looked no older than me, spoke up

'Well, don't look so frightened, is this your first time?'

I looked closely at her. Though about my age, she had eyes that were much older, knowing eyes that betrayed a tougher life than mine. She was dressed as one might expect: a see-through blouse and very short skirt. I looked around the tiny room, mainly occupied by a double bed with crumpled bedclothes. I assume they didn't change them between customers. There was little else: a wash basin, dressing table, mirror. It was all very seedy. The girl was looking at me now, awaiting a response. I knew immediately I wasn't going through with it.

'Sorry, this is all a misunderstanding,' I said. 'I thought I was going to a party.' I didn't wait for her reply, but rushed out of the room. Once in the corridor outside, I turned the opposite way to the one I came in through; I didn't wish to meet the others again. I ran down dark, deserted corridors till finally I found a stair going down. It led me eventually to a backdoor, but when I tried it was firmly locked with no sign of the key. In desperation, I tried a room off it whose door was slightly ajar. It was some kind of junk room, but there was a window. I tried to raise the sash, and fortunately it opened and I scrambled through. I was now in a small back yard, completely enclosed by a brick wall. But there was a gate out, and I slipped through it and into a back alley. I raced down it, as I still feared someone might come after me, offended by my rejection of the house's custom, or wanting payment of some kind. But no-one did and I wandered out into a narrow street, just like the ones we'd come through earlier. I was totally lost, and so stopped for a moment to regain my breath, unscramble my brain and make some plan. I decided that if I headed just in one direction, I must hit a main road sooner or later, and then I could get to a tube station. But this strategy proved more difficult in practice than I imagined. Each time I tried to keep to one direction, I was forced into ninety degree turns, or got stuck in a cul-de-sac and had to backtrack. Finally, I reached a pleasant square, with a garden in the middle, and large imposing Georgian townhouses all around. And at last I saw someone. He was on the opposite side of the square, sitting beneath a statue of some 18th century worthy. There was something familiar about the figure, and long before I reached him I knew who it was.

'Stephen, it's good to see you.' Considering he seemed totally lost and must have been for ages, he was in surprisingly good humour. 'It's most kind of you to coming looking for me.'

I didn't disabuse him. 'Come on, Giles, let's get home, shall we?' That of course was easier said than done, since neither of us had any idea where we were, but he immediately had a simple faith in my ability to achieve that goal.

'I knew I could depend on you, Stephen. I knew it would be you coming after me, not Huw or Piers.'

'Huw did go to look for you', but he didn't hear. We set out down the most likely road out of the square, and soon saw lights and traffic at the end of it. We were back on a main road, which turned out to be Gower Street. We headed up to the Euston Road. I looked at my watch. The coach back to Cambridge had gone; we'd have to take the train, if there still was one. So we walked the short distance to King's Cross Station. A look at the departures board soon told us the depressing news that there was no train till the morning. There was no option but to spend the night in the waiting room. As we approached it, a familiar figure was already there.

'Hallo, Huw', said Giles. 'You missed the coach too.'

'Trying to find you, boyo. I looked everywhere. And what have you been up to then Stephen?'

'Oh, looking for Giles, too,' I said mendaciously, hoping Huw would not press the point. But he just grunted, and went back to reading the Tribune. We settled down to wait for the milk train. As the sky lightened, and the train was almost due, another young figure came on to the platform, looking as bright as the proverbial new penny.

'Well, good morning, boys, surprised to see you here. Would have thought you'd be back tucked up in bed by now.'

We were all too tired to respond, and, after that initial sally, Piers seemed as tired as the rest of us. I was relieved no-one asked him where he'd been, and he made no comment to me about the events in the brothel. Once back in College, I went straight to bed, and didn't awake till later that evening. I imagined the activities of the night before would be soon forgotten, but in that respect, I could hardly have been more wrong.

The next morning, Piers joined me for breakfast. He rarely made it, so I guessed he had a good reason for being there.

'Stephen, dear boy, I would be grateful if you did not say too much about our exploits in Soho. Let's keep that as a secret between ourselves.'

'Don't worry. I'm hardly likely to advertise the fact, especially as Giles thinks I was out looking for him. But the only exploits that night were by you.'

'Yes, you did leave rather suddenly. I'm sorry about that; maybe it was a step too far for someone of your bourgeois background.'

'Don't be so patronising. You obviously aren't too proud of it, or you wouldn't want me to keep quiet. And it was really quite sordid. I'm amazed you thought it was a good idea, especially when you have a girlfriend like Penny back here.'

He just smiled. 'Ah, yes, respectable monogamy. It might interest you to know Penny is not quite so virginally pure as you think. She likes a bit on the side as well.'

I looked at him in amazement. Though Jo had hinted such a thing already, I had largely discounted it as bitching. The idea that Penny might be sleeping around came as a total shock. For a moment, I could think of nothing to say. Then a most unworthy thought entered my head; perhaps I might have a chance of sleeping with her. I suppressed it immediately. Piers saw my confusion and laughed.

'I do like you, Stephen. You have such strong principles and morals, without being totally unworldly like Giles, or a bore like Huw. I'm sure they will prove very comforting in your future life, though they'll stop you enjoying much that life has to offer. Me, I'm quite immoral, I'm afraid. If it's fun or intriguing, I'll give it a go.'

I smiled in return. 'Yes, you're probably right. We can't escape our nature.'

'But what is our nature? My mother married pater because he was of the right caste and had land and money. They never loved each other, and by the time I could notice they led separate lives, each with their own lover. If I'd grown up in your household, would I be a different person?'

For a brief moment, I felt I was getting through to the real Piers; that there had been an epiphany in our relationship. But the gap in the curtain closed; there were no more revelations…

Chapter 13

Suddenly I was brought back from my memories. At first, I was disoriented, something was wrong but I didn't know what. Then it struck me and I realised why I had snapped back into the present: all conversation on the table had ceased. I looked at the faces of Piers and Arthur opposite; they had gone white. I slowly turned and then I saw. Having just entered the Hall, and standing by what was clearly his place, was Giles.

He had changed a lot, thinner, leaner, and harder as well. The soft naivety that had typified him all those years ago was gone. He was grey now, of course, and his face had, not surprisingly, a similar pallor, the effect of years confined. His dinner jacket could easily have been the same size as he had at college, if he'd ever owned one. It was second hand, as if it had come from a charity shop. No production of the Scottish Play could have induced such a shock amongst us, but this was no ghost, Giles was very much flesh and blood.

Huw broke the silence. 'Well, boyo, I didn't expect to see you here.' Even his voice wavered.

'No, I'll bet you didn't. No greetings then, lads. The spectre at the feast, eh.'

He brushed aside our speedy mumbled apologies. 'It's OK, lads. Considering the circumstances, it's hardly surprising you wouldn't expect or want to see me now. But strangely, once they let me out, despite everything I wanted to see the old college again. And yes, see you all. Because you are where things finished. My life stopped, and you are all I have to come back to. I saw you were all down for this reunion and I couldn't stay away. After all, the Famous Five would not be complete unless we are all present.'

He sat, and hungrily devoured his starter as we silently watched.

'How long ago were you...?'

'Released? Oh, a few years ago now. I'm considered cured, now. Safe to be let out. But they still keep an eye on me.'

'It must have been awful.'

He issued a mirthless laugh. 'Oh yes, it was awful alright. At first, anyway. It got easier as the years went by. Looking on the bright side, I suppose it could have been worse. It was all hushed up, of course. No trial, unfit to plead, no-one wanted the scandal, and with my record of instability, my suicide attempt, well, not difficult to justify that I did it 'whilst the balance of my mind was disturbed'. So no publicity, I became a non-person. Everyone preferred to pretend that I'd never existed. Including you lot.'

'Where were you ...'

'A secure mental hospital, at first anyway. At least it had nurses rather than warders, though they were pretty burly blokes, not exactly angels of mercy. It was bad at first, not quite padded cells and straight-jackets, but pretty close. Things got better over time. Some of the other inmates seemed normal, many were intelligent. I became friendly with several of them. One guy I got on really well with, he seemed a normal bloke, except he'd taken a cleaver to his father, because he'd been possessed by the devil. I got used to the enforced communal life; it wasn't too different to being in college.' He laughed at this point, and took a swig of his wine. 'I worked in the library, helped other inmates with their education, even tutored them for OU exams. Finally, I was quite respected, especially when I explained.'

'Explained what?'

'Later. I haven't had a meal as good as this for a while. It tends to a bit more basic in the hostel.' He saw our faces. 'Well, what did you expect? Think I could just pick up my life after all that time with my record? Think I would be an MP, or a housemaster, or a successful author. Oh yes, I've followed all your careers. It's amazing what you can find on the internet.'

'But, you did do it, you were guilty…'

He paused in his consumption of the excellent steak, and took a sip of wine. 'Ah, that's good. I bet you've all been drinking wine like this for years. Maybe you find it bland and boring; you should try the hooch we brewed inside. Now that was an experience, and it certainly helped to make the living easier, better than the happy pills, anyway. But as you were saying, I must be guilty, because I wouldn't have been locked up otherwise, would I? Certainly, it was convenient for all of you, helped you to get on with your lives, put all the unpleasantness behind you.'

'That's not really true, old boy', said Piers. 'It's left a mark on all of us. None of us was ever the same again.'

He looked at our expressions, and burst out laughing. 'Suffered, did you? God, none of you were in a high-security mental hospital, in the company of psychopaths some of whom would kill their own mothers and in some cases had.' Then suddenly his mood changed. 'Of course, this is no chance reunion. You're all here to discuss it, to persuade yourselves that really it wasn't you at all. Nothing to do with you, all totally innocent.' He banged his knife on the table, so loudly that those around turned and stared. 'Well, you could hardly have the circle broken. All five of us were there, and we are tied in the circle forever, as you'll find out. Yes, you'll all hear the truth tonight, whether you want to or not.'

The meal progressed in silence, and I found myself becoming more and more detached. Half the time I was here, and half the time back forty years, the faces of the other four melting and reforming like in a Malcolm Bradbury novel, sometimes young, enthusiastic and hopeful, sometimes old, grey and fearful. Whether it was my preoccupation with what was to come or the effect of the College cellar wine I don't know, but the later proceedings – the speeches by the Master and the journalist – passed me by. Then we were all standing for a toast to the college: Floreat Collegium, or something like that. Then the High Table departed and I knew it could not be put off any more. We adjourned with the rest of the alumni into the Schofield Room, named after an eccentric don from our time, famous for wearing open-toed sandals in all weathers. Huw as always was the most practical and brutal.

'I think it's time, boyos. Let's get down to business.'

Piers grabbed a bottle of brandy put out for post-prandial drinks. Some of the other alumni looked indignantly at this, but a glance at our expressions silenced them. He led us out through a labyrinth of corridors till we came to a baize green door. Magically he produced a key – 'got it when I was doing some research and never returned it' - and we went in. I realised we were inside the library; there was no light but some illumination creeping in from the court below highlighted the book stacks. We went to a table between two rows, and pulled up chairs. Piers and Arthur were on one side, Huw and I on the other, Giles at the end. Piers opened the bottle of brandy and filled up each of our glasses. There was a silence now; the five of us sitting in the dark, no-one wishing to start. Then Huw spoke up.

'Come on, let's get started.'

We each took a strong swig of the brandy and silence reigned for a few seconds, then I spoke up: 'I'll begin.' All murmured assent. I took another swig of my brandy, swallowed, took a deep breath. The memories swept in…

The first intimations of impending disaster came a week before. We were all well into finals by then. The University still insisted on the old rules, and we all were dressed in our gowns as we arrayed ourselves to take each section. I hadn't worn mine much over the three years, so it wasn't in too bad condition, just incongruous with the long sleeves and short length, quite different to the master's gown I purchased later, a last-minute acquisition from Ede and Ravenscroft for a school speech day. I don't know what happened to it. I recall little of each exam, except the inevitable tension. Each went surprisingly fast, so that time was called, it seemed, almost immediately after I picked up my pen. We all sat in the traditional rows somewhere in a hall near to Queens'. We heard stories of those who had buckled under the strain, of students collapsing and being taken to the local hospital and the like. There was only one incident out of the ordinary that I recall in mine; a rather flamboyant examinee with long flowing blonde locks, who arrived late, and stayed only a few minutes before leaving in as abrupt a fashion. What happened to him I never knew.

Giles was seated a few desks away from me, and his presence was strangely reassuring. He seemed to be doing well, and that comforted me strangely. It wasn't just that I still felt protective towards him, but in an odd way his industry was a talisman. As long as he was doing well, then so must I be. Therefore, it came as a shock when about the third or fourth exam he suddenly did not appear. I expected him to arrive at the last minute, and even when the invigilator started the exam I expected him to come in, flustered but all right. But that didn't happen. When the exam finished I hurried back to College, heading for his room. On the staircase, I met Huw. One glance at his face told me everything.

'They've taken him to Addenbrookes, boyo. I'm heading there myself now.'

'What, whatever's happened?'

'He took an overdose. Fortunately, the bedder found him in time and called an ambulance.'

We both raced down to the bicycle racks and pedalled furiously down to Addenbrookes, then situated in Trumpington Street. It's a business school now, and there's a restaurant in out-patients! We soon located where he was; it wasn't visiting time but we talked our way in and got to his bedside. He was sitting up, looking pale, but otherwise well. As we arrived he turned his face towards us, and smiled, rather sheepishly I thought.

'It's good of you to come and visit me.'

'How are you?'

'Oh, I'm fine now. They pumped me out, which wasn't very pleasant, but I feel OK now.' He spoke in a very matter-of-fact voice, as if he'd eaten something that had disagreed with him. I cut through the inhibited atmosphere.

'What on earth were you thinking of. Don't you realise how much you worried everyone?'

He seemed genuinely surprised by my comments, as if it had not occurred to him how anyone might react, or how much people might care. That upset me most of all, I think, that despite our friendship he might do something like this without telling anyone.

'Why didn't you tell us what was wrong? We're your friends, not just casual acquaintances. We could have helped.'

He looked away at that point. 'No, you couldn't. Thanks for saying that, and coming, but you couldn't help me.'

I persisted: 'But why? You still haven't said why.'

He smiled; a thin rueful, knowing smile that said, 'you should be able to work it out.'

'I'm feeling rather tired now. It's been a traumatic day; I'd like to get some rest. Thanks again for coming.' He turned on his side, away from us, and it was clear the visit was at an end. We left the hospital with very mixed emotions. We were pleased that he was clearly not in danger any more, but upset that he wouldn't tell us what was wrong, or let us in at all. As we cycled sombrely back to college, not speaking at all, I realised that this was the start of the end for all our friendships. As the end of our Cambridge time approached, we all had ignored the implication for our relationships. There was a tacit agreement not to discuss it, but now as I steered between the traffic to swing into the College, I knew the friendships would not last, no matter what we might say or indeed wish. This was the end of our student world, the end of the Famous Five. It didn't matter what happened now;

Giles' attempt had succeeded in killing our collective friendship.

I thought we would not see Giles again, but amazingly the next day he appeared in hall, pale and rather withdrawn, but there in person nevertheless. We gathered round supportively, greeting him over enthusiastically, as if he had returned recovered from a disease or accident rather than a self-inflicted crisis.

'You look much better, Giles. How are you feeling?'

'I'm much better, thanks. Oh, and thanks for coming in to see me in Addenbrookes. I know I was boorish, but I did appreciate it. It definitely helped my recovery.'

We didn't enquire again as to why he did it, and to this day I don't know why, though subsequent events offered some sort of explanation. I asked him about his plans.

'Are you going home now?'

To my surprise, he turned to me with an angry fire in his eyes. 'No, I can't do that.' And then for the first time the façade broke and he blurted out 'I've let them all down, can't you see that. It always mattered more to them, and I couldn't live up to it'. He seemed on the verge of tears, and without another word walked away. We were silenced; there was nothing we could say or do. I felt it was the low point of my time at Cambridge; little did I know what was to come. I didn't say any of that. It wasn't relevant to what happened, at least not in the semi-judicial way we had decided to proceed. I decided to concentrate on the day itself. There was no problem in recalling it; the important moments were engraved on my memory.

It had all started so well. The day was a beauty: hot, perfect blue sky, it was as if we were back in Edwardian

Cambridge, before the Great War, and like those long-forgotten undergraduates we little knew what was to befall. It was the day of the College May Ball, the climax of our post-Tripos celebrations, the day we would always remember. That was true of course but not the way we expected. Piers, Arthur and I were going. Huw of course did not approve.

'Total waste of money. And sealing the College off! Talk about elitist!'

I had some sympathy with his views; it did seem a bit Brideshead, but the girls wanted to go and that of course tilted the scales. Piers was going with Penny, and I of course with Jocasta, Arthur with a girl from Girton who sang. We had hired dinner jackets for the event, and spent what little was left of our grants to buy the tickets. The girls had all bought or been given long dresses, had their hair done specially; it was the social climax of our Cambridge sojourn. We were all in and out of each other's rooms as we got ready in college, the girls changing without embarrassment as well. I remember Penny in her underwear, looking someone to help her put on her dress.

'Come on, Steve, you can help me, Piers is so into himself, he's no use at all.'

As I zipped her up, I felt her skin, so soft, smelling of perfumed soap. She turned.

'You do love touching my body, don't you, Steve?'

It was like that day in my room, a tease, part innocence, part come-on. I blushed deeply and she laughed. She broke away and spun round twirling her dress.

'Look, Piers, aren't I perfect.'

I turned to Jocasta, hoping she had not noticed my embarrassment, but she was looking spellbound at Penny as well. We were all captivated by her, then, it seems strange now, but that's how it was. Eventually we were all organised, and we joined the queue of couples going into the ball, our tickets ready. It was a mass of colour: every conceivable colour of dress draped in stoles of silk or fur, all off set by the severe black and white of the men in black tie. Music was playing inside the quadrangle - it was a well-known jazz band – there were lanterns everywhere, photographers taking preening couples, waiters handing out glasses of champagne. We wandered around, the six of us together, taking in the atmosphere: the sounds, lights, smell of perfumes. A magical feeling, I can still conjure it up, especially if there is a trigger, like a whiff of scent, a bar of jazz, a flash of colour. It must have been like that in the past, those legendary days before the Great War that I've already alluded to, but there was something else, a lack of inhibition, the spirit of the 60's, a sexuality rampant that wouldn't have been there in past generations. And also, there was a classlessness, despite the evening clothes, a sense that protocol and etiquette did not rule. We were not all from the same strata of society, where everyone knew each other and memories would be long. Within days we would separate forever, this was a last chance to enjoy Cambridge and freedom, before careers and family intervened. Tonight, anything might go.

We drank a glass of champagne each, and then went in to our dinner sitting. The Hall was like a fantasy, lit with candles, with a choir playing, surprisingly reminiscent of tonight's dinner. I can't remember much about the meal; it was a salmon salad I think, finishing with strawberries and cream. All I do recall is that our glasses were regularly filled. We occupied our own table, with another couple who I can't now even recall. I do remember that there was a tension between Penny and Jo. I don't know what started it, but the finale stuck in my mind.

At some stage I went off on my own to find the lavatory, and there to my surprise beside a table dispensing drinks were Huw and Giles.

'What on earth are you doing here, especially after all you said.'

Huw gave me a knowing grin and touched the side of his nose. 'Ah, but we haven't paid, have we, Giles. No, we are upholding the rights of collegers to go wherever they please. And drinking compliments of the toffs, present company excepted, of course.'

I looked closely at Huw's outfit. He had on a pukka jacket and bowtie, albeit ancient and ill-fitting, but he was just wearing ordinary dark trousers. He saw my expression.

'Got the jacket at a jumble sale. There were trousers but they didn't fit.'

Giles seemed better shod; perhaps he had borrowed the kit. But I didn't look too closely at that; it was his expression that held me. He looked, how do the Celts express it, fey. There was an other-worldliness about him. He said nothing, but was clearly now totally under Huw's spell. I couldn't stay; I'd already been away from the others a while.

'Well, good luck to you. Keep away from Torquil and company; they'll have you thrown out. Enjoy the rest of the night.' I conducted the business I had originally set out for, and then tried to make my way back to the others. It proved much harder than I expected. I realised I'd drunk more than I had intended, and things were starting to spin a little. Everything was breaking apart, there were couples snogging in corners, some girls running in tears, loud voices, drunks lying on the grass. It was early in the morning, long after the meal and the restrained dancing of early evening. The Lord of Misrule was free and passing amongst us, fuelled by bottle after bottle of champagne. Anything might now happen. I couldn't find the others, and ended up eventually in front of the Master's Lodge. Suddenly, there in front of me was Penny.

'Found you at last. Where are the others?'

She said nothing, but just looked at me. She had a strange look, a mixture of come-hither and triumph. She also looked more beautiful that I had ever seen her.

'I don't where the others are. Do you really want to find them?'

It was a clear invitation. Before I could answer she came close and put her hand beside my face.

'Remember what I said in your room. It wasn't right then, but it is now. Last chance, Steve. Last chance to have me, what you've always wanted.'

I was drunk, of course, but that was no excuse. I think I would have done the same even if I had been sober. She took me by the hand and we went to a gate beside the Lodge. Beyond it was the garden. It had been used during the evening, but now it was pretty deserted, just some empty tables, some drunks or couples lolling on seats. We went across the lawn and into an area that wasn't lit, where we were totally alone. We embraced, kissing passionately, thrusting our tongues deep into each other's mouth. She was wearing a shoulder less dress, and I unzipped it, remembering that I had zipped it up only a few hours before. I ran my hands over her breasts, and she pulled me down onto the ground beneath a tree. It was a pine of some kind and the floor was littered with pine needles, which gave a soft bed. Her breasts were free now, and I touched them for the first time. They were soft to the touch, so much softer than Jocasta's. She was tugging at my waistband until it came undone, and she slipped her hands inside. I pulled up her dress, and down her knickers, very brief if I remember correctly. She gave a gasp, partly of pleasure, partly of triumph.

'Oh yes, Steve, yes, all the way. You couldn't resist me, could you?'

I knew I couldn't say all that. I gave an expurgated version, leaving out seeing Huw and Giles, and all the conversations, and especially what she said to me.

'…it was barely lit; I can't even recall if we were allowed in there. Few were about, as I recall, and even fewer were compos mentis. We crossed the lawn together hand in hand. Neither of us was saying anything, but our purpose was clear. Would I have done it if I wasn't drunk, if I'd not argued with Jo, if it hadn't been the end of our Cambridge careers. To put it bluntly, I wanted to shag her, and all inhibitions, all social restraints had gone. We slipped behind some bushes, sure no-one could see us, but perhaps not really caring. We were kissing, I felt her body, her breasts, she was feeling me, as keen as I was. We lay down on the ground, her dress had ridden up. I remember, incongruously, her knickers: white, frilly and brief.

'Go on, Steve, you know you want to…'

Then I was on top of her and in her. I didn't care where I was, what I was doing, this is what I'd wanted to do since that first day in Lensfield Road. I was spent and I rolled off and looked up. There were Piers and Jo, looking down. Piers spoke, in a voice I'd never heard before.

'We wondered where you'd gone, were looking for you...'

I could say nothing, Jo was in tears; all I can remember was Penny laughing, uncontrollably, contemptuously...'

I stopped speaking. There was a silence that seemed to go on forever. I reached out and took another swig of my brandy; then I went on. 'That's it, that's my part. I ran out of the garden and back to my room. There I stayed till the next morning, when the police came round. I told them I hadn't seen Penny since before midnight. Once I'd made a statement, I packed my things and went to the railway station. I have never been back to the College since then, till now.'

I sat down. We looked around; who was next? After a tense silence, Piers stood up.

'It was as Steve has said. I'd got separated from Penny and was looking for her. I bumped into Jo. She was distraught, looked as if she had been crying.

'Have you seen Steve? I'm worried about him, we argued and I'm afraid he'll do something stupid.'

We looked together around the courts, and then bumped into Arthur.

Arthur interjected then. 'That's right. I'd met Steve and Penny together by the Master's Lodge. Steve seemed very drunk, and Penny seemed weird. She was dragging him almost, towards the Master's Garden. When Piers and Jo

came, I made a mistake I've regretted every day since then.'
He fell silent.

Piers continued. 'He told us Steve and Penny were in
the Garden. We went in after them. It wasn't difficult to find
them; they hadn't made much effort to hide themselves, and
the sounds made it very clear what was going on.'

It was strange to hear me being described in the third
person like that, but perfectly apt, as if we were in a trial, and
every detail had to be meticulously recorded.

'Steve fled, dressing as he ran, and Jo and I stood
looking at Penny. She was lying on the ground, triumphant,
arrogant. Then Jo said, 'Two can play at that game.' She
grabbed me, and kissed me full on the lips, nothing held back,
like a wild woman. Somehow we fell back against a tree, and
then her legs were wrapped round me and her dress round her
waist. And then Penny was hitting me, screaming, out of
control. I pushed her off but she was punching and scratching
at me. I put my fingers round her neck and squeezed, till she
stopped struggling and went limp.'

There was total silence, a dreadful brooding silence
that we thought would never end. Then from somewhere
came a hollow mocking laugh.

'So that's what you think. Have you carried that guilt
all these years, Piers? That's sad. Perhaps that's why your
novels are so dark. Trying to wash away the guilt in stories.
Though you weren't upset enough to come forward, were
you? You were happy for me to take the rap, weren't you?
No, the great Piers couldn't end up inside. Well, don't worry,
Piers, you can rest easy now. You didn't kill her. She was
alive when I found her. Just regaining consciousness.' Giles
stood triumphant, in total control, all of us frozen to the spot.

Eventually I broke the spell. 'So why did you kill her? Why? I've never understood that.'

'Oh, surely not. It had to be me, didn't it?'

'What do you mean by that?'

'It was so convenient for all of you. I was always the outsider, the one you had to watch, the one who was different.'

'That's not true, Giles.'

'Oh, yes, it is. I know, Steve, that you think it isn't, that you were protecting me. It came through, you know, without anyone having to say it. I was your good turn, your charity. Keep Giles safe, poor unworldly Giles, who couldn't be trusted on his own, poor Giles, the one you felt sorry for.'

'That's not true, Giles. Totally untrue.'

He turned on me with a vengeance. 'Oh yes, it is, Steve. I was a convenient scapegoat for you, someone who was worse than you. So you didn't have to confront your own inadequacies.'

Before I could make an angry retort, Giles jumped in. 'At least Steve cared. None of the rest of you did. You only really cared for your music, Arthur. And you for your politics, Huw. I was part of your poor bloody infantry. Or maybe a 'useful idiot'. And as for you, Piers, you really hated all of us, didn't you? You always thought you were better than us.'

There was a silence in the room. Then Giles turned to Huw. 'Go on, tell your part now.'

For once Huw seemed tongue-tied. Then, in a surprisingly hesitant voice he began. 'Well, boyos, I have to confess; I was the reason Giles was there. I hadn't intended to go, of course, not approving of such displays of privilege.

But then I was chatting to one of the College servants whom I knew, not someone most of you would have even noticed, but we'd become friends over the time we were up. He told me of a sure-fire way to gatecrash the ball, involving back doors, unofficial master keys and a bit of climbing. The whole thing appealed to me, cocking a snoot at the posh prats. I got myself a second-hand dinner jacket and a dickey bow. Telling Giles about it was a spur-of-the-moment thing. I felt he needed something to get himself out of his depression; it would be a bit of a giggle, a way of getting his own back I suppose. He seemed very keen, so come the day of the ball we were properly attired and ready to go. I so regret it now, but could I have anticipated what would happen?

We got in with no trouble, and initially enjoyed the thrill of gatecrashing. We both drank lots. I remember bumping into you, Steve. We were nearby when you and Penny slipped into the garden, and we saw the whole incident. It was a laugh to begin with, but then it started to turn nasty. So I left the garden. And the ball, the whole thing had gone sour.'

Someone from the darkness said, 'did you see Giles...?'

'No, I had left by then. Like Steve, I didn't know what had happened till the next morning.'

A silence. Then someone said, 'there's just one person to hear from...'

'Yes, it's my turn.' Even in the darkness, I could sense every face turning towards Giles. His voice resonated in the blackness of the library. It had a strange authority; that I'd never heard before in Giles. He had us waiting on his

180

every word, and, like a veteran actor, he had his audience in the palm of his hand.

'I've never really told my story. Not in court, not to my family. But now is the time. That's why I came tonight. Sorry to disappoint you all, but it wasn't to celebrate our 'friendship'.' Suddenly his voice rose. 'Not one of you came to visit me, not one of you contacted me, not even you, Piers, who'd thought he was the killer. Not you, Steve, who so prided himself on caring for me. And not you either, Huw, who was the reason I was there at all. None of you deserve to hear anything, but I need to tell someone, so it's your lucky day.

Let's start at the beginning. I'd come up to Cambridge with such hopes. First in my family and all that. The age of meritocracy. Earned my place through my brains. I thought we'd all be equals; this was a brave new world. Boy, was I to be disappointed.'

His language was different, his whole personality. His experience had certainly changed him; he was, strangely, more confident, more assertive. And there was a quality he had that none of us possessed. I struggled to understand what it was, and then I knew. Feral. That's what he was, feral. There was a sense of danger about him, a chill, almost a fear, and yes, almost a respect, for someone who had gone somewhere no ordinary mortal goes, and survived an ordeal, the fear of experiencing which must haunt all comfortably brought-up, law-abiding citizens. We listened in stunned silence; the smell of almost tangible fear mixed with an all-pervading magnetic force that made us hang on every word.

'I soon realised that there was a pecking order, laid down over the centuries, and you all slid effortlessly into it, all except me. I was always the awkward squad, the one that didn't fit. Oh, don't deny it,' he asserted as a slight ripple of dissent disturbed the atmosphere. 'Piers was at the top, and he got the prize, Penny. You hated that didn't you, Steve? Oh yes, I knew. Poor little naïve Giles, I knew exactly what was going on. It was like the Middle Ages. Piers was the lord of the manor, you were the loyal retainer, Arthur, and you were the yeoman, Steve, the honest broker, the one who always smoothed the way, filed off the rough edges. And Huw, you were the revolting peasantry, always there, ready to be used where necessary, no real threat to anyone. I was the only revolutionary amongst us, the only one who wanted real change. And you took it on yourself to deal with me, Steve, the way your class always has.'

'That's more than a little unfair', I said. I did really care for you, wanted to keep you out of trouble.'

'Well, you didn't do a very good job, did you? But that's enough psychology. Let's get back to what happened that day. As you know I'd discharged myself from Addenbrookes after the overdose. Did I really want to end it all, I'm not sure? Perhaps, but an overdose is always a dodgy way of topping yourself. Much more certain jumping out of a window.' He laughed at the shocked expressions on our faces. 'That's upset you, hasn't it? Taken you out of your comfort zone. Believe me, I've been well out of my comfort zone these last few years.'

He stopped for a moment, and took a sip from his glass. The silence was so intense we could feel it; it seemed to be weighing all of us down. Giles looked up, and smiled grimly at our expressions. 'I'm glad you're all ears. Well, once I got back to college I'd no idea what I was going to do.

I couldn't go back home; I'd failed them all, you see. So I remained in college, lasting out the few days left to me at Cambridge. No idea what I'd do next; it all seemed quite hopeless. No future at all. Maybe left to my own devices I'd have had another go, who knows?

Of course, I had no intention of going to the May Ball; that was the last thing on my mind. I knew of course that you, Piers, Steve and Arthur were going, and you, Huw, was not. Therefore, I was amazed when you came to me and said you were going to gatecrash it. That immediately appealed, cocking a snoot at the authorities, taking off the toffs in our makeshift outfits. It was easy to get in from the college; they obviously hadn't thought that their 'Gentlemen' would do such a caddish thing. At first it was fun, drinking the free booze, laughing at the pompous antics. But it soon paled. It reminded me of all the reasons I hated Cambridge. I was just about to go when it all got interesting.' He stopped, again, just for another sip. Then he was silent, as if wondering if he should go on. But he put down his drink and continued. 'Suddenly Steve was there, and Penny. There was clearly chemistry; she was strange, almost fey, I'd never seen her like that before. When the pair of you went into the garden we shouldn't have followed, but we did, and saw the whole thing, 'in flagrante', the lot. I'd never seen a couple doing it before, nor since for that matter; it was voyeurism, but strangely quite satisfying, at last the established order was broken, the lord of misrule was abroad. Huw scarpered: I think there's a puritanical streak to you, Huw, you weren't comfortable at all. But I stayed and saw it all. I saw Piers arrive, and his hands round her neck. But as I said, Piers didn't kill Penny.'

He stopped, and took a long draught of his drink. We waited for him to go on, but the silence stretched out, and eventually we all realised he was going to say no more. I couldn't hold back any longer.

'So, did you kill Penny, or not. You've got to tell us.'

He turned and I felt him smiling in the darkness. 'Did I kill her? The police and the lawyers and psychologists certainly thought so. But that doesn't make it the truth does it. I think you know in your hearts who actually killed her. You don't need to hear from me.' Without another word, he got up and left the library; his steady steps resounding on the stone staircase, gradually disappearing into the silent blackness. I never saw him again.

Chapter 14

When I awoke the next morning, at first I was totally
disorientated. I was in a place I knew, but then again I didn't.
I reached out for my wife, but she wasn't there, of course. I
was in a single bed, back in Bradley's, back in my old room.
And it was familiar still, even without the books on the
shelves and the poster of Ursula Andress on the wall. I lay
back and savoured it. Over forty years since I'd last slept
here, here in the bed where I'd lain with Jo, clasped tightly
together on the narrow mattress. The years fell away and I
remembered it all with total clarity.

I also remembered the night just gone, the sudden
emergence of Giles, the confessions, the revelations, the angst
of forty years played out in the gloomy netherworld of the
Library. I realised also that it had solved nothing. I still
didn't know what exactly what happened that day, though it
was clearer than it had been. I looked at my watch: seven
o'clock. There wasn't a sound from the others in the nearby
rooms, but I didn't want to remain in bed. I jumped up,
pulled on a pair of shorts and went downstairs to shower.
That helped to clear my head, which was just starting to
remember how much I had to drink. I dressed and set out to
walk. I knew I had to get out of the room: too many
memories, too many images in my mind. I crossed the Cam
and headed for the back gate, which fortunately had already
been opened. I headed out away from the centre, down West
Road, past the Choir School and the Sedgewick site, past the
rugby ground, till I was clear of university buildings. Just
playing fields and farms. It was worlds away from the

university and the College, peaceful and deserted. I sat down, my back against the gate and let the late September sun, still warm this late in the year, beat on my face. I closed my eyes, and let my thoughts run wild.

One thing that came across, Giles was clearly saying he didn't do it. That amazed me as much as it had the others. I'd always taken that as read, and thought our guilt lay in letting things go as far as they had. But maybe there was someone much guiltier, someone who had let an innocent man take the rap, as they say. But could that be true? Why had Giles confessed if he didn't do it? Didn't most murderers claim they were innocent? But then they did that at the beginning; if Giles did do it, why should he lie or try to mislead now? And if he didn't do it, who did? It certainly wasn't me. Which one was it: Piers, Arthur or Huw? As I wrestled with my thoughts, I knew at the back of my mind there was something I'd missed. Something crucial, some small fact that would slip into place and finish the jigsaw. But try as I might, nothing would come into my mind.

I got up and started walking back towards the College. Things were coming back to life; I saw a tractor in a field and a couple of cars passed me. When I got back to the Queens' Road crossing, there was even a tourist bus disgorging its cargo. I was in an uncertain frame of mind; I wasn't sure I wanted to see my friends, but knew I had to. I went into the server, which looked like a kitchen, and ordered just juice and toast. Then I took them into the Hall, already cleared from the feast, and sat on one of the long trestles just as I'd done on the first day. And there, just as he had been all those years ago, was Huw.

'Well, boyo, that was an interesting evening.'

'Yes, I still can't get my head around it. Did Giles really say he didn't kill Penny?'

'I never thought he did. I thought he was covering up for someone. In fact, boyo, I thought it might be you.'

'Me? Why on earth would you think that?'

'You two always seemed to have a special relationship. You were always trying to protect him, as if you were the younger brother. Why shouldn't he have repaid the debt?'

I really didn't have any retort to that. 'Well, whatever his motives, I didn't do it.'

'I didn't say you did. But you must admit, you were somewhat fixated on the girl. We could all see it.'

'So why not Piers then? Or maybe you. You played your cards close to your chest. I don't remember you having any girlfriends, or expressing any interest in anyone.'

'I had a girlfriend back in the valleys, boyo. Didn't see any reason to expose her to the collective attentions of the Cambridge illuminati. And I did suspect Piers. I thought Giles might well be protecting him, in fact I thought there might be a relationship between them, or an unrequited love.'

'Piers and Giles! Don't be silly.'

'Oh yes, Piers is certainly gay. That was a part of the problem. It was always a phoney relationship with Penny. He wanted cover, and she wanted the contacts. Networking, they call it now, don't they? Yes, that was part of the problem.'

I sat there stunned. So much of this had passed me by. Huw got up and turned to me.

'Well, I have to be going. Got to get back to Westminster, or the whips will be fretting. It's been good to see you again. Maybe now we can meet again, as the ice has been broken.' He held out his hand, and after a brief moment of hesitation, I grasped it. He picked up the tray and was just about to leave when he turned back to me.

'I was a bit harsh on you there, boyo. I didn't 'really' believe it was you. I think we both know who it was, if we really think about it.'

Before I could reply he was gone. I finished my breakfast and took the tray back, my mind still on what he had said. I didn't feel like seeing anyone else, so I went back to my room and packed as quickly as possible. Before I departed I took a last look at my set. The ghosts still hung heavy there; it was as if I could smell Penny's perfume. For an instance, I saw them all as they had been: young, alive, the world in front of them. I turned and slammed the door, and went down the wooden staircase without looking back. I got back to my car without seeing anyone, and soon was on the Madingley Road heading towards the motorway. It felt just like the day I'd left before, in my father's car. No looking back. But as I drove I thought on Huw's words. What did he mean: that we all knew?

Chapter 15

I was almost back when it came to me. How could I not have seen it before? I remembered the day on the punt. It was obvious now. As I entered the school grounds I knew it all. She was waiting for me as the car pulled onto the gravel in front of the house. As soon as I saw her expression I knew I was right.

'It was you, wasn't it, Jo. That's why you didn't want me to go. You strangled Penny. She was coming round when Piers had gone. Then she laughed at you, didn't she? Perhaps called you a whore. Perhaps she'd done that before. She'd shattered your world, humiliated you once too often. You'd seen what Piers had done, and you did the same, but this time till she could breathe no more. Did Giles come when you'd finished, or did he watch you doing it? He was in love with you, wasn't he? I think I knew that day on the punt. And when he took the blame, you knew it could all be rescued. Penny was gone; you were safe. And we could resume, with me guilty for ever.'

Jo smiled grimly. It seemed she had aged visibly in the time I'd been away. There was a resignation about her; she wasn't going to deny it. Perhaps it was a relief to finally tell someone.

'But you were always the catalyst. It all happened because of you. I knew you wanted Penny, but I loved you. I always feared she would steal you from me, just to show she could. I hated her all the time we were there, and killed her many times in my mind. I don't regret it; she was a bitch.'

There was a silence.

'So what happens now? Are you going to turn me in?'

'Turn you in for what. One of us has already paid for her death; changing that would make the sacrifice worthless. In some ways, we've all paid. This has blighted our lives ever since. In a strange way, Giles is the only one who's got release. And besides, that happened in another world. There were people at Cambridge called Steve and Jo and Giles, but they don't exist anymore. They're just memories.'

I put her arm around her, and she leant against me. 'It's almost time for evening prayers.'

'Yes, I'd better take them. I've imposed enough on our house tutors whilst I've been away.'

'Wilkins minor wants to talk with you. I think it's to do with his parents…'

Forty years on, when afar and asunder

Parted are those who are singing today,

When you look back, and forgetfully wonder

What you were like in your work and your play,

Then, it may be, there will often come o'er you,

Glimpses of notes like the catch of a song –

Visions of boyhood shall float them before you,

Echoes of dreamland shall bear them along,